Freakn' Out

Out

(Freakn' Shifters, Book Seven)

Eve Langlais

Copyright © May 2016, Eve Langlais
Cover Art Amanda Kelsey Razz Dazz Design ©
March 2016
Edited by Devin Govaere
Copy Edited by Amanda L. Pederick
Line Edited Brieanna Robertson
Produced in Canada
Published by Eve Langlais ~ www.EveLanglais.com
1606 Main Street, PO Box 151
Stittsville, ON ,Canada, K2S1A3

ISBN-13: 978-1533465221
ISBN-10: 1533465223

Chapter One

Kill it!

The scorpion scuttled across his path, the pointed stinger poised in a high arch over its segmented back. Nasty buggers. They could cause quite the sting. At camp, if you spotted one, you immediately killed it. Squish! Boot stomped hard. Yes, it would make a crunchy wet noise. And, yes, some of the veterans liked to mock the fresh faces by faking little screams when a newbie had to make his first kill. The expression on their faces? Priceless.

The critter scampered close, but this one time, Derrick let the scorpion live. Why not? Out here in the middle of who the fuck cared, it wasn't likely he'd run into it again. Besides, lifting his foot would waste some precious energy. He needed every ounce he could get.

The sun beat down on his helmet, and the sweat pooled, rolling in thick rivulets to soak the collar of his shirt. The harness straps dug into his shoulders, yet he dared not shed those supplies—a canteen, knife, and other crap deemed necessary for survival. In this arid land, so far from home, with the rules not the same as he'd grown up with, every advantage was needed.

The terrain he and the other soldiers crossed proved merciless—the hard ground leached of moisture, the very air itself beyond parched, every inhalation bringing with it a faint patina of dust. The fine grime existed everywhere, layering the air even along the outer perimeter of the slow-moving convoy. A utility vehicle led the way, sometimes speeding ahead before stopping and waiting for them to approach, their advance scout watching for danger.

Derrick initially had begun this trip riding in a vehicle, but it didn't take long before the hairs on his neck began to rise. When they stopped to give everyone a break, the lieutenant in charge of this convoy asked for some walkers to scan the outer edges, as the next few clicks were considered the most dangerous. Derrick immediately volunteered. However, the initial enjoyment of stretching his legs soon paled under the beating sun.

The rumble of a large diesel truck, a dusty brown and gray with a tarped rear, revved as its driver got impatient at the slow pace. It wasn't as if they needed speed for their mission. Sent on a supply run by his superiors, he and the other soldiers protected a caravan of food for the refugee camp, along with miscellaneous supplies. Getting there alive and with their goods was more important than how quickly. It never failed to amaze Derrick the amount of shit needed to keep a camp going, whether it be military or civilian.

I have a much more intense appreciation for toilet paper. As a matter of fact, when his tour eventually ended and he returned home, he was going to fill a room with the softest ass wipes he could find. Floor to ceiling.

Chuckle.

Boom!

The explosion took him by surprise. The deafening noise hit his ears before the ground rumbled underfoot.

Shit! Someone had hit a landmine. Even as he dove to the ground, he already knew it was too late. A few objects impacted against his back, and he couldn't stop a hiss at the sudden searing heat. Struck by shrapnel, the loose bits of metal packed around the bomb. They made for deadly projectiles when mixed with explosives, but at least he lived, if face first in the dirt.

He'd hit the ground and bounced hard, slamming against the gritty soil, grinding it against his lips. Faintly, through the ringing in his ears, he could hear shouting, the faint muffled yells of others caught in the backlash.

"Joey's down. Medic. We need a fucking medic."

"My leg. My leg. My leg," screamed another.

In Derrick's case, it was his back. It throbbed in a spot high on his shoulder, the burning piece of metal an alien thing his flesh protested painfully. Lower though? Although he knew something had hit him there, he felt nothing. Perhaps those pieces had bounced off.

As another explosion shook the ground, he ducked his head between his arms, covering it from the raining debris.

Such a fucking cowardly way to attack, and not how he wanted to die. *We walked into a trap.* A trap he'd never even smelled because they bloody buried it and his nose was almost useless with the grit muffling his senses.

Hate the sand. His wolf ever did whine for

them to go home. His more canine side missed the crisp freshness of a forest and the soft verdant nature of a field filled with soft grass.

He missed the smells of home, but he missed more not being able to count on his most refined skill. His nose usually led him away from danger, but out here, his extra special sense proved useless, and that meant difficulties when it came to easing himself from the active minefield, where any wrong step could blow him up.

Except I'm not supposed to walk on a suspected minefield.

During their training and conditioning exercises, Derrick and the other recruits were run through dozens of drills. At the time, some of them seemed surreal, like the one their grizzled instructor claimed might, "Avoid getting your sorry asses blown into bite-sized chunks."

Some of the guys said the minefield test was what separated men from the dog food. The key was a slow, and with little pressure, crawl out of the danger zone. He'd passed that exercise no problem, so it should be a cinch now.

I hope.

Derrick pushed himself up on his forearms, ready to creep from the minefield, except his legs didn't seem to want to cooperate.

What the hell? Had something landed on him, pinning him without him knowing?

A glance over his shoulder showed nothing there. Even more frightening, there wasn't any pain, not a sensation at all.

Gulp. Perhaps he'd just gone numb? He struggled to bring his knee up. Wiggle his toes. Feel or move any goddamned thing below his waist.

Nothing.

I can't feel a thing.

Panic gripped him, clutching him tight in a fist and taunting him. *I'm paralyzed.* The very idea horrified him, but he quickly reminded himself it was not the end of the world. Chances were his infirmity was temporary. Once he made it to a hospital, they'd fix him up. Shifter genes were stronger than human ones. They healed quicker and better from most wounds. He tried to keep that hopeful reminder as his mantra instead of recalling the soldiers who'd gone home before him. Broken men in body and spirit.

As Derrick clawed at the dirt, dragging his body—*my useless fucking body*—across terrain that still trembled as a chain reaction set off other bombs, he tried to remain optimistic. *I'm gonna get out of here. Doc is gonna put me on a few days bed rest and tell me how lucky I am. Maybe I'll get a pass to visit home. Have a beer with my bros.*

He just needed to make it to safety and that could happen. Find himself a hidey hole while he waited for the military to pick him up and take him to a field hospital for a little shrapnel removal.

Just stay alive. Stay alive amidst the smoke and dust that hung in the air, a heavy fog that did nothing to muffle the screams, but hid their attackers, who suddenly started firing.

Fuck. This was more than just a random attack with IEDs. Actual rebel forces had lain in wake and now ambushed. They were even more dangerous than scorpions. Their arrival made getting to a better defensive position even more important.

Claw and pull. Dig those fingers, grip with those tips and heave. He pulled his overly large—*damn my healthy large-boned genes*—body forward, but it took effort. Panting with exertion meant drawing in the dirty air around him and then coughing, short, sharp exhalations.

Perhaps it was that sound that drew attention, or someone got lucky with a random shot through the murk. The sharp projectile skimmed across his skull, dragging a furrow in his scalp.

"Mother fucker." The expletive burst from him, and he could almost imagine the taste of the soap his mother would have made him eat if she'd heard it. Such a strange memory to flash on and the precursor to pain. It arrived with prompt sharpness as blood drizzled, hot and wet, from his temple. Sticky, cloying stuff. He could see nothing through the eye he had to shut while the other blinked at the dust stinging it.

What a sight I must make. Not his finest moment.

Through the cotton bells that both rang and muffled his hearing, he caught a shrill plea for mercy. "Please don't kill me. I've got a w—"

Bang.

The begging ended mid-word. A systematic execution by the enemy. If they were killing soldiers, then Derrick was done for. Toast. *I can't escape.*

His inner wolf didn't agree. With a snarl, it shoved at the bond that held it prisoner inside his head. Shoved and got nowhere. It wasn't the one in charge. Derrick reminded his beast of that.

What will you do as a wolf? Snarl and snap at them?

8

Apparently, his beast saw nothing wrong with that plan, not even the sure-fire bullet to the brain. Once again, his other half pushed. Oh how hard his beast pushed for control, enough that Derrick had to make an effort to remain in the driver's seat.

I can't believe you're making me fight you. But he won. A win that might be short-lived as Derrick heard the crunch of boots on the ground, approaching from behind. He rolled to his back, determined to face death like a man.

A wolf would tear out death's ankle, his wolf thought in a full-blown sulk.

The infidel stood over him, brown woolen scarf hiding the lower half of his face, another piece of it covering his hair. A head fully hidden except for cold, dark eyes.

There's a look I recognize. Of course Derrick knew it, as he saw it on the face of every enemy he met. The rebels fought for their version of justice. Derrick would find no mercy here, and he wouldn't ask for any.

A sneer tugged one side of his mouth. "What are you waiting for, asshole? Shoot me." Taunt thrown, the fingers of Derrick's left hand curled around the handgrip for his pistol. He'd slipped it from the holster when he rolled. Now he just waited for his chance.

The fellow raised his rifle, the round black hole of the tip staring Derrick in the eye. At point-blank range, his chances of survival weren't looking good. With no time left, Derrick lunged upward, pulling his gun out of hiding.

There wasn't much time to aim, but his target

stood fairly close. The gun fired, the retort sharp and his aim steady, considering. What Derrick had not expected was how not being able to flex his ass to hold himself upright would screw him over.

He'd practiced shooting one-handed enough times to expect the recoil, but that was when his whole body worked. He landed flat on his back, the motion jarring enough that he lost his grip on the pistol. Hopefully, he wouldn't need it again.

The guy, who thought he'd have an easy time executing Derrick, arched as a red flower blossomed on his chest. The infidel shouted out in alarm and stared down at his chest in disbelief, but only for a scant moment. With a yell that Derrick was pretty sure was the translated equivalent of, "You're dead, dirty fucker!" he brought his rifle back to bear, even as his life force pumped from his chest wound. Before he could shoot Derrick, another voice barked, more guttural consonants that Derrick didn't understand. The result? No bullet to the head or any other body part.

That wasn't reassuring. If they didn't want him dead, then that meant they wanted him—alive. He'd heard stories and had no interest in living some of the more vivid ones.

Derrick rolled to his side and looked for the gun he'd dropped as the shouts neared. He could practically feel the vibration as boots hit the ground in a run nearby.

He couldn't find his weapon before several bodies surrounded him, all wearing their version of combat gear and those feature-concealing scarves. Of more concern, they were armed to the teeth, and as Derrick knew, none of them were squeamish about shooting an injured man on the ground.

Except, instead of filling him with bullets, they did something worse. They took him prisoner because, as his captor explained in broken English, "The best prisoners, they no run. You no run." Big smile. The most chilling words a man could hear. They wanted to torture him for information.

They were quite good at it too. With them, Derrick learned pain he'd never imagined, especially once they began to marvel at how well Derrick healed. To their sadistic delight, he quickly healed most of his injuries, except the one affecting his spine. The shards embedded in his body, poisonous metal threaded with silver, kept him from repairing his biggest weakness.

But that was his only weakness. When it came to pain, Derrick was a pro. All shifters were, and Derrick wasn't the type to reveal secrets. *I'll die first.*

His captors tried their best, though, and they questioned and questioned and… Derrick said not a word, and he took their punishment. Took the pain and didn't crack. They employed every technique they knew. He had the scars, the ones gouged with silver, to prove it.

But I didn't crack.

The torture didn't last as long as some others suffered. Perhaps two weeks all told, yet it was enough. When the military finally rescued Derrick from the camp where the rebels held him captive, he was a shell of himself, a broken and dirty man who snarled at everyone, even those who would help him.

In order to survive, he'd relied on his beast a

little too much. Let the wolf protect him from the worst. Returning to the man he had once been proved...difficult. Derrick was no longer the brash and fit soldier who set out to do his duty for his country. He rolled off the plane a cripple, a useless veteran who couldn't even take a proper piss—or jerk off a quick one in the can.

More than once he wished the infidels had killed him. Killed him so he wouldn't have to live like this. A burden on everyone.

I won't do it to them. I won't do this to my family. He spared them that chore by throwing himself at the mercy of the military who had a place for guys like him, some kind of rehab center for broken soldiers—many of them shifter ones. Derrick thought of it as the farm people sent their broken pets to die.

Not exactly the most uplifting place. A handful of angry men, frustrated men with wild eyes and, in some cases, snarling beasts. Throw in the occasional livid woman sporting sharp claws. They were supposed to support each other, and some of them did, but Derrick kept himself apart, segregated because he wasn't like them. Something was missing inside him. He knew it. He hadn't completely come back from that rebel camp.

Within, his beast paced, caged and yet pushing to get out. Pushing to take over. It would be so easy to let him take over.

And tear off the face of the guy who is practically doing cartwheels in his new prosthetic. Show off. Derrick envied him so hard. He could have handled having metal limbs. Better than what he got stuck with.

He thumped a closed fist down hard on Meat

Snake One and then on Meat Snake Two. Didn't feel a thing.

Argh.

"Should you be doing that?" a dulcet voice asked. Stupid lack of privacy. The open door to his room at the rehab center didn't prevent anyone entry, nothing to stop the stranger from simply strolling in and bringing a tingle of awareness with her.

What's happening?

Every small hair on his body lifted, and he sniffed.

Smells good. Real good. *I want it. Have to have it.*

Not it. Her. Want her.

No. Oh hell no. Disbelief swelled within as he smelled *her.*

It wasn't that the woman who entered smelled bad. On the contrary, she was beyond divine. Flowers was his first thought. Springtime tulips, red ones with the bright yellow centers exuding a spot of brightness in the dreary and breathing freshness into the world. She smelled of renewal. Life.

She's smells like mine.

No.

Lifting his gaze—which the mirror showed still glinted more wolf than man—Derrick leered at the chubby redhead in the ill-fitting blouse and slacks. Such a delectable morsel. A sweet thing sent in to collar the beast. Didn't those treating him and keeping him caged know better than to put someone so innocent, so delicate, so *human*, within reach?

Grab her. She's ours to take.

How long since he'd taken a woman? Long

13

before the accident even, probably not since his last leave home, as fraternizing with the local girls was frowned upon.

So a long time since he'd fucked. He obviously suffered from overfull balls—balls he could no longer drain—and here the administration sent temptation—and a reminder of his impotence—to taunt him.

Did they want him to snap? Was that their plan? Did they know how much it would hurt to see a woman, such a desirable woman, and know he couldn't do a fucking thing about it?

Cruelty to animals. Bite their face off.

Used to the violence, he ignored the suggestion, but knew he had to do something to get the woman out of here. Since the shrinks wouldn't do the right thing and lock him up—they kept insisting he could adapt when all he wanted to do was chase them through the woods—then Derrick would have to do the next best thing and scare her off before he did something he could never take back. *Like tear the clothes from her succulent body and dive between those creamy, curvy thighs.*

The erotic visual served only to remind that licking was all he'd ever do again. His days of fucking and satisfying a woman were gone.

I am not a man anymore. And he was never more reminded than when the woman who could have been his mate—and lover—entered his room. She needed to go. Now.

"Hello, darling," he drawled. "How nice of the military to send me a snack. I've been ever so hungry for a woman." He snapped his teeth at her and rumbled, a low, menacing, and, yes, slightly inhuman sound.

To his surprise, she didn't recoil from his threat. Instead, she leaned forward and smacked him on the nose with a rolled-up folder. To add insult to her ignoble act, in a no-nonsense tone she said, "Bad wolf. Behave yourself right now, or there will be no treats for you!"

Say what?

Chapter Two

The surprise in his eyes was quickly masked, but at least she managed to catch his attention. Good, because she needed to set the tone early.

But Derrick wasn't done posturing for dominance. Janine's newest patient leaned back in his wheelchair and folded his hands over his flat stomach as he perused her, his glance taking in her appearance from her hair, simply brushed and pinned back with a barrette, her clothing—ill fitting due to a mishap with her luggage—and her face bare of makeup. He stared at it all, especially where a button threatened to pop at the top of the straining blouse.

If he thought to intimidate, he'd have to do better. She took stock right back. A big man, his shoulders stretched wide while his arms were corded with muscles. Despite his infirmity, Derrick kept himself fit. According to the verbal summary she'd received, Derrick spent several hours a day working out, keeping his upper body in shape. As for his lower body…her gaze went to the legs that only massage kept from atrophying.

According to his medical reports, a piece of shrapnel in his spine was to blame, its position considered too sensitive to operate. The worst part about the incident was, according to her superior, had he received immediate medical attention after the attack, he might have recovered fully, but the time he spent in enemy custody gave the metallic sliver a chance to work itself deeper and then flesh healed around it, encasing it. Its buried presence left a man in his prime handicapped.

The paralysis of his lower limbs didn't take away from his looks. On the contrary, even seated in his chair, Derrick exuded virility and power. The man was ruggedly handsome with dark hair, sinfully sexy brown eyes with thick lashes, and sensual lips that shouldn't be drawn into such a thin line of disapproval.

"Are you done staring at the cripple?"

"Are you done staring at my boobs?" she said, pointing out his inordinately long gaze at her cleavage, which practically fell out of her shirt. With her luggage lost between her car and the room assigned to her—*"It's got to be here somewhere,"* someone assured her—she'd had to borrow, and the fit didn't exactly flatter.

"If you don't want your tits stared at, then maybe you shouldn't have them hanging out."

His remark called for a peek downward. "I hardly call less than an inch of cleavage hanging out."

"And I say it's inappropriate. Gonna smack me again for stating the truth?" he snapped.

She shrugged. "Only if you deserve it." For a moment, she wondered if he'd do something on purpose to make her react. Bring it. She was more than ready for it.

Instead, the challenging fire that had risen to the surface of his gaze for a moment dimmed. "I don't know what your game is, lady, but I'm not playing it. There's the door. Use it." He dismissed her.

Someone attempted to assert control. Problem was Derrick's idea of control included shoving everyone away, especially people who wanted to help him. But Janine didn't plan on leaving.

I am a woman on a mission. A job, to be more exact, hired to handle Derrick's case for several reasons. One, she was considered top in her field when it came to cases of post traumatic stress disorder and helping victims cope with infirmity. The even bigger reason why she got head hunted for this case? She happened to know shifters were real. Real, furry, and often pig-headed, even if they tended to growl, not snort.

She took the few steps needed to reach his door and shut it. As she turned around, he rumbled his displeasure. "I thought I told you to leave."

"Not until we talk."

"I don't want to talk. Find yourself someone else to harass."

"Too bad. I choose you."

His eyes flashed for a moment, pain lighting them before the hardness returned. "Choose someone else."

"Or you'll what? Go big bad wolf on me?"

"I don't know what crazy pill you took today, but perhaps you should have worn a strait jacket instead of that blouse."

"We both know I'm not crazy." Perching herself on the edge of his bed, she placed her hands on her knees before leaning forward. "You can drop the act. I know what you are."

"And what is that? A pathetic dog? Isn't that what you inferred? A man who is no better than a lowly pet who must beg for treats with good behavior? Fuck you. I don't need this kind of bullshit."

"I see I'm going to have to be more blunt. I know you're a shapeshifter. A wolf, to be exact. One with"—she peeked at the file she'd placed on the bed beside her—"five brothers and a sister born of Meredith and Geoffrey Grayson, also wolves."

If she'd thought him angry before, he was now even more coldly so. "Who are you, and how did you get this information?"

"Finally, he asks the right question. I'm your new doctor, one sent by the council, I should add." There was no need to elaborate. In the Lycan world, there was only one council that mattered, the high one that governed all of shifter kind. The one her stepdaddy happened to serve on, but she didn't share that fact.

"Like fuck did the council send you." He spun his chair around and wheeled it across his open room, sparsely furnished with only a bed and nightstand. A television was mounted to the wall, but he had nothing else lying around. Not a single photo or book. Nothing of a personal nature. The room could have belonged to anyone—or no one.

"If you don't believe me, then call."

He spun around quickly, his strong hands easily maneuvering the chair. "Call? Just like that. Are you trying to tell me that a *human*"—a word sneered with contempt—"has a direct line to the council? I call bullshit."

"And I think you should curb your language.

You are in the presence of a lady." She angled her chin. While she didn't actually mind the foul words, one of the steps she found effective was reminding her patients of the basics, starting with manners. How could he expect to treat himself right if he didn't respect others?

"Lady. Hmph." He made a disparaging noise. For a moment, he stared at her.

She allowed it and didn't move. One of the things she'd learned over the years working with the wounded, especially wounded shifters, was to never show fear. Ever.

In the shifter world, a wolf like Derrick held a predator status. It automatically meant certain behaviors were ingrained. For example, predators could smell weakness. It made them want to assert their dominance. Right now, Derrick really wanted to assert himself as the one in charge, but if she allowed that to happen, she would never get through to him. He would forever see her as beneath him.

To throw him off balance, she pretended as if he didn't peruse her with the intent to possibly eat.

Although he does have a mouth made for sinful pleasure.

Such an inappropriate thought, and for a patient no less. Standing from the bed, she took the few steps that separated them and held out her hand. "Perhaps we should start over. My name is Janine Whelan. I'm a clinical psychologist for a private hospital a few hours from here. I've been tasked with helping you to reintegrate into society."

He didn't take her hand, rather glared at it. "I'm Derrick don't give a fuck who doesn't need any help because I'm fine."

She arched a brow at the lie. "So fine you haven't seen your family since your return to Canadian soil. So fine you've refused all visits from them. So fine you'd prefer to whine about your plight instead of learning to adapt to life with it."

"I am not whining."

"Then why won't you see anyone who cares for you?"

"Because I don't want their pity." He snarled the words. "I don't need them looking at me and saying 'poor Derrick.'" He pitched his voice for emphasis.

"Caring about you is not pity."

"Isn't it, though?" A sardonic lilt of his lips said he thought otherwise. "I know what will happen. I've seen it before. They'll treat me like I'm useless. Fetching me shit I can get for myself. Curtailing their normal activities so I don't feel left out. Warning people not to stare."

"They might do these things, but it wouldn't be malicious in intent."

"No. But it's emasculating. I don't want to be treated differently."

She verbally slapped him. "But you are."

A hot glare lasered her way. "Thanks for the reminder."

"You can stop throwing visual daggers. If there's one thing you will have to get used to, it is honesty from me. And that honesty includes me saying, yeah, you're not like everyone else right now. A part of you is broken, and you're learning to adapt, and to those who've never experienced it, it will seem different. You can't change that."

"Great pep talk, Doc."

"It's called getting you to wake up. To stop being a coward."

The incredulous look on his face wiped the scowl. "You're calling me a yellow belly? I've seen and survived shit you can't imagine, Red. Shit that would make you piss your pants. So you can take your fucking fancy-schmancy mumbo jumbo and fuck off."

"Given your record, I can't believe you are too chicken to chitchat with me."

"Fuck you. It is not cowardly to not want to talk about my feelings and dissect every last thing that happened to me. I don't need to relive my time in that prison. It sucked. Sucked sweaty, hairy donkey balls. I don't want to talk about it. I just want to be left the fuck alone."

"That's not going to happen."

"It would if you left," he growled.

"Being alone is not an option. Not for you. Maybe you could get away with it if you were truly alone in the world without a soul to give a damn about you, but I've got a list of people who care about you. People who are tired of you shoving them away."

He turned his head, his bearing tense. "My family is better off not seeing me how I am now."

"Better off?" She snorted. "I call bullshit." She knew the vulgar word would grab his attention. When used sparingly, it had an effect. "This is how the world is, Derrick. In the real world, when people get hurt or sick, then it's normal for those who love you to want to help. Yes, it might be help you might not need. Yes, you might not want it and have to deal with some staring, but tough titties. Sometimes, you have to suck it up, stop being a princess, and accept the good intentions for what they are." When she was done with her rant, she was almost panting, having feared that taking a millisecond to breathe would give him the chance at a rebuttal.

Instead, he blinked. "Holy fuck. Exactly what kind of head shrink are you?"

"The best."

"Sent by the council?"

She nodded.

"And here I thought they didn't give a shit what happened here."

"They care more than you know." This rehab center might be military owned, but it was operated mostly by shifter sympathizers, in other words, shifters and humans in the know. Because they couldn't entirely control who came here, though, the patients were a mix, so discretion was still required.

"What if you can't fix me? What then? You wouldn't be the first to try and fail."

"I won't fail." She couldn't fail this broken man because she was his last chance.

He peeked at his wrist and the watch strapped there. "Sorry, Doc, but I gotta go. Ben, my trainer, is expecting me."

"You should get going then. I just wanted to pop in and introduce myself. I'll see you tomorrow."

He spun his head to glare at her on his way past. "No I won't."

"Yes, we will. Ten a.m., here or in a common area. It's up to you."

"If you want to talk to me," he muttered as his hands gripped and pushed the wheels, "then you can bloody well find me. It shouldn't be too hard.

After all, you have your legs to use."

A rude ending to their first session, but it wasn't Derrick's lack of manners that bothered Janine most. It was her reaction to him. A reaction she'd never had before.

In all the years Janine had treated patients, she always managed to maintain a professional detachment. The people who came to her—or that she went to see by special order—needed help, and she provided it. She prided herself on giving them what they needed, whether it was tough love or understanding.

With prickly Derrick, she already knew what method she would use. Any hint of softness toward him and he'd clam up. She'd lived through that once before with her dad, her real one, and that was the reason why she became a clinical psychologist in the first place.

Since she'd gotten her degree, she'd counseled her fair share of wounded warriors and traumatized people. Derrick might seem tough, but she'd sort him out. What worried her was how attractive she found him.

When he talked, she found herself fascinated by the movement of his lips. He ranted, and she wanted to grab him by the scruffy cheeks and kiss the anger from him.

Totally wrong. Wrong. So wrong. He deserved better than her fantasizing so inappropriately. Her attraction made her wonder if she was the best person to deal with him, and she told her stepdad so during a phone call, minus the whole lusting.

She paced the confines of the room they'd

given her for her stay in at the rehab center. "I don't know if I can get through to him, Orson. He's bitter and lashing. Don't you have a guy who can take on his case? I'm not saying Derrick is chauvinist, but I don't think me being a woman, and a human one at that, is helping things."

"Don't you think we tried a male first? More than one actually. Derrick has sent every single last one of them packing. You're his last hope. If you can't get him to calm down…"

Her stepdad trailed off, and she frowned. "What are you worried about? Do he think he's suicidal?" She'd not gotten that impression. Angry, yes, but she got the sense that at his core existed a fighter, and she'd not sensed the dangerous despair—not yet at least—that overtook so many other soldiers suffering from PTSD who also had to deal with the new reality of a physical impairment.

"Derrick's a loose cannon right now. Worse than that, he's a hurt animal. And animals who are in pain, even the mental kind, do stupid things. Crazy things. Things that might reveal secrets best left hidden."

"You think he might go wolf in front of people?"

"He partially has a few times. Luckily, they know about us and won't talk. But his lack of control is a problem."

Of course it proved a problem because if Derrick lost control, there was a chance he might go *feral,* a term used when the beast took over. "You're afraid he'll out your kind."

"Perhaps not knowingly, but yes. He's not in his right mind, and unless we can get him back on a leash, we might have no choice but to terminate him."

"Terminate him?" She couldn't help but yell the words, the very implication shocking. "He's not a freaking dog or cat. He's a person."

"And a wolf, June-bug. Never forget that. He might look human, but inside lurks a beast, and should that beast break the chains holding it, there's no telling what it will do."

No, it wouldn't be good if the big bad wolf came out. Not good at all. Shifters survived because they managed to keep the secret of their existence hidden. If the world at large were to discover they existed, even she wasn't so naïve as to believe the two species could coexist in happy harmony. Fear tended to trump common sense and compassion.

So she understood her stepdad's position, but that didn't mean she would let it happen.

I will get through to you, Derrick Grayson, whether you like it or not.

Chapter Three

"I don't like it," Derrick complained to his surgeon as he lay face down on the table. He'd grown to gruffly respect the older fellow, a doctor who seemed to think if they could remove that last bit of metal in his spine, he might, just might, get some use of his legs back. Or the operation would fail horribly and leave him a human potato head with no movement at all.

With that kind of fifty-fifty chance, he hesitated. Life was hard enough now. He couldn't imagine it getting worse.

"What's not to like? I saw the new doctor when she was getting set up with her access badge. She's a cute thing. I wonder if she's as fiery as her hair."

The growl rumbled without thought on his lips.

The doctor misconstrued his agitation. "You don't like her type? Sure, she's a little curvy, but personally, I like a plump lady."

So did Derrick, but that wasn't why he growled. He didn't appreciate the fact the doctor noticed her in the first place. If he didn't know better, he'd accuse himself of jealousy.

Because she's mine.

Oh no she wasn't. She couldn't be, and yet, the certainty lingered, a certainty that came from deep within. It emerged from the wilder part of him, a part that since his incarceration seemed to think *he* could express himself whenever he liked. At times, the loss of control frightened Derrick. His wolf wasn't supposed to be able to push past his psyche and react. His wolf shouldn't constantly try and nudge him aside to take over.

Perhaps if you let me out, I wouldn't shove so hard, was the thought his beast retorted with.

Let his wolf out and risk never getting back into his skin? Derrick hadn't dared shift, not since the accident. It wasn't just his dominating wolf that worried him, but the fact that the violence of the change might shift the last bit of metal in his body.

He fidgeted on the examination table, realizing the doctor still waited for him to reply. "I don't have a problem with her looks." On the contrary, he liked them a little too much. "It's what she's here for that bugs me."

"And why do you think she's here?"

"To make me a happy, smiley asshat who pretends he doesn't give a fuck he's a cripple. Why the fuck can't people just leave me alone? I'm handling my shit the best I can."

"Are you?" the doctor questioned.

"Have I missed any appointments with you or my physio dude? Nope. Not a single one. And just ask Ben. He'll tell you I work like a fucking dog. I'm not slacking, and I'm way ahead when it comes to doing the things I have to in order to drag this useless body around."

"Your body is not useless. You are perfectly capable of leading a full life, even with your injury."

"A full life that involves pissing through a

fucking tube. An awesome life watching porn instead of making it. Yeah…" He uttered a bitter laugh. "My future is so freakn' awesome."

"And with that kind of attitude, you really have to wonder why they sent you another clinical psychologist."

He did wonder, and he did chafe. Surely a man was allowed to wallow a little bit in self-pity, and he'd earned his right to some anger.

"Did you feel that?" the doctor asked.

"Feel what?" Still face down on the table, wearing only his briefs, the only thing he felt was the light breeze coming from the air vents, teasing along the skin of his back.

"What about this? And this?"

Derrick had to peer over his shoulder to see that the doctor pressed various parts of his legs and feet, seeing if anything reacted. Nope. Nothing behaved as it should below the waist, not since the explosion.

Broken. Howl. He didn't let the insanity inside his head pass his lips.

He faced forward again as the doctor kept palpating his dead flesh.

"How are your bowel movements going?" the doctor asked.

Long used to these types of questions, Derrick knew better than to avoid them. "Fine. So long as I keep to my schedule, I haven't had any accidents." Instead of resorting to a diaper, Derrick chose other methods to void himself of waste. Yet another reason to not let friends or family get close. No one needed to know about the hour he spent each morning and night on the toilet doing what came naturally to everyone else. No one needed to know the indignity of the catheterization he had to endure several times a day so he wouldn't wet his pants.

The threading of the tube in his flaccid cock each day only served to remind him how dead he truly was. More than a few times, he'd slapped his dick and screamed at it, angry that it too betrayed him. Life would surely suck less if he could at least jack off.

I'm an impotent male in his thirties who is a step away from wearing diapers, and that stupid head shrink wonders why I can't go back to my old life.

Shame was a powerful thing.

So was desire, yet even his interest in the red-headed doctor wasn't enough to get a rise. Not even a twitch, goddammit.

Perhaps he should count that as lucky. Most shifters who met their mate entered something more commonly known as the mating fever. It meant they had to have intercourse with their *one*. If they didn't, then their desire would turn them wild. Literally wild. A horny predator looking for some pussy wasn't something the world needed to see.

What surprised him was the smack of recognition when he saw the curvy doctor. With his cock more useless than tits on a bull, he would have thought himself immune from the mating urge. What stupid fate would pair a broken man with a nubile woman?

"Have you given more thought to the surgery?" the doctor asked. "Your latest x-rays show that the fragment has shifted. I'm afraid if we don't do something soon, it will do more damage."

"Care to remind me of my odds?"

The doctor sighed as he took off his glasses and pinched the bridge of his nose. "You know I'm not going to lie, Derrick. It's not looking good, whether you do the surgery or not. If you do, then there's the chance your condition will worsen, and if we don't…"

"I'll get worse. Or die." Was it wrong to hope for the second part?

He couldn't bring himself to do the brave thing and kill himself. Just couldn't. But at the same time, he couldn't take the chance of surgery leaving him even worse off. At least now, he had a semblance of life. He could, as folks kept reassuring him, rejoin the populace at large and eke out an existence.

Or go on a killing spree. If only they would let him have a gun.

But they didn't. Assholes.

"Do me a favor, Derrick, and at least think about the surgery."

As if he did anything else. He'd thought about it, long and hard, but in the end, his fear of becoming a quadriplegic emerged stronger than his optimism it would work.

Fear proved to be a powerful force when left unchecked. It had him hiding the next morning from the doctor.

I don't want to see her. Didn't want the reminder of what he couldn't have.

Unfortunately for him, and despite her human nose, she tracked him down.

Chapter Four

Expecting Derrick to duck out on their session meant Janine was ready and waiting for him the next morning. She stood outside of the building he was housed in and kept watch. Sure enough, about a half-hour before their session was set to start, the front doors to the building opened with an electric whine as someone pressed the automated button.

Derrick emerged, hands wielding the grips of his wheelchair, pushing himself along at a quick clip, so quick she practically had to trot to keep him in sight. She knew better than to confront him in the open. Besides, she wanted to see where he went.

The rehab center grounds housed numerous buildings, most of them for rehabilitation of some sort. While they offered an in-house program for people like Derrick, they also took those who had adapted enough to function in the outside world but still needed a place they could exercise.

Derrick bypassed the gym facility nearby and followed the road, never once peering behind. His route was by no means vacant. She found it interesting to note that Derrick didn't ignore the waves of those he passed, giving them a brief salute of acknowledgement. Perhaps not as antisocial as he wanted to claim.

Wheeling his chair suddenly to the right, Derrick's destination soon became clear, an outdoor pool surrounded by a chain-link fence. The gate yielded to a swipe of his keycard, and she slowed her steps as he parked his chair. He still hadn't looked behind him. Did he know she followed? He certainly didn't act as if he did. Were his usual predatory instincts dulled by his injury, or did he just not want to acknowledge her?

She halted at the gate, mesmerized by the glimpse of skin as he pulled his shirt off. He tossed it on a bench lining the fence. For a second, she couldn't see much, the straight back of the chair hiding Derrick as he bent forward to remove his track pants and shoes.

Stripped down, he then rolled his chair to the edge of the water and set the brake. A little more maneuvering, which involved the straining of his upper body as he hauled his weight from the seat to the edge of the pool. She had a moment to see the scars on his back, red whorls, still fresh and probably silver based, and other scars, silvery ones that had healed but left marks.

Before she could examine the rest of him, he sank into the water. And she meant sank.

Uh-oh.

Sprinting along the fence line, she made for the gate, only to slam hard into it, rattling the chain links when it wouldn't open. She spent a few annoying and precious wasted seconds swiping her access card across the lock sensor, the buzz and click meaning she had access. She flew through the gate, kicking off shoes as she went, ready to dive to the rescue, only to stumble to a halt.

Piercing eyes met hers as Derrick, submerged to his nose, glared at her, his arms stroking the water and keeping him afloat.

He rose enough to mutter, "What are you doing here?"

"It's a nice day for a swim," she said, perhaps a tad too brightly.

"Or a drowning. Because that is why you came rushing in here, isn't it, Red? Thought I was going to end it all by sinking like a rock to the bottom."

"Can you blame me for the assumption?" She arched a brow. "After all, we do have an appointment that you chose to skip."

"It's not ten yet."

"Don't split hairs with me. We both know you had no intention of keeping it."

"So you followed me."

"I did."

"And let me ask you, if I really had decided to drown myself, exactly what makes you think you could have saved me?"

Her chin tilted. "I'll have you know I spent two years working as a lifeguard for our local pool. I am fully qualified to save your life."

"Thing is, Red, what if I don't want you to save it? Isn't a man allowed the choice of living or dying?"

It was a question she often heard, especially by those still dealing with debilitating injuries. Stuck in a pit of despair, they couldn't see the light, the possibility. It was up to her to drag them out. "I think everyone should have the choice. My job is to make sure you don't decide without all the facts or too hastily."

"I have all the facts. And some of them

blow." He dipped under the water, and big bubbles rose to the surface. This time, she didn't panic. Instead, she rolled up her pants legs and sat on the edge of the pool, dipping her feet into the water. Only to snatch them out and yell, "That's freakn' cold!"

He burst from the skin of water, water clinging to his lashes. "That's not cold. It's invigorating."

Tucking her feet under her, she shook her head. "Only if you're a penguin. Do you swim in this arctic pool often?"

"Every day unless someone is bothering me." The intense glare made her smile.

"Don't mind me. I'll just sit here and watch. We can talk when you're done."

"What if I don't want to talk?"

"Then I'll keep following you around until you do."

"Will you wipe my ass when I go for a shit?"

"No, because you're a grown man and you can wipe it yourself."

"If I'm a grown man, then why aren't you respecting my choice to not have my feelings analyzed?"

"Because."

"That's your argument?"

She smiled. "If you want to know the real reason why I'm forcing the issue, then I guess you're going to have to talk to me."

"Are you always this tenacious?"

"My stepdad says I have the tenacity of a bear after honey."

"Perhaps you should try mimicking a bee and

buzzing off." With those words, he sliced sideways into the pool, arms pumping as he stroked through the water in a front crawl. The liquid helped a bit with his leg situation, giving them some buoyancy, but she still knew how hard he had to pull in order to stay afloat. It made her wonder who authorized these swims without supervision.

Then again, chances were Derrick chased away anyone who tried to treat him as if he needed a keeper to watch over him.

The man appeared more prickly than a porcupine, but Janine considered it a point in her favor that he'd not yet driven her away.

Since Derrick seemed determined to ignore her for the moment with his swim, she dragged her phone out of her pocket. No surprise, it blinked at her. More text messages.

The first one was from her mom: *Hey, June-bug. Don't forget the big anniversary party at the end of the month.*

As if she'd forget. Twenty years was something to celebrate, especially since after the death of her dad, Janine had worried her mom would never find happiness again. Mom blamed herself for Janine's dad's suicide. They all did. It had taken Janine many years to realize it wasn't her or her mom who were at fault for her dad's sink into despair. Daddy had needed help, was even offered it, but he'd refused it, and when things became too much, he took the only way out that he thought was left.

Why, Daddy? Why did you leave me? The cries of a daughter abandoned still haunted her to this day.

Janine made it her mission in life to see that

no other child ever had to suffer like she had.

She fired a quick text back to her mother. *Of course I haven't forgotten. I was planning to get there a little early so we could chat before it starts.* Which would require her leaving the medical facility mid-afternoon the day of and driving just under three hours. But at least she could spend the night. She'd sublet her apartment because of her projected tenure here. Her contract had her locked in for three months minimum, more if necessary. But she was lucky. If she needed a place to go, then she could go home. Unlike other parents with empty nests, her mom and stepdad kept Janine's room intact and encouraged her to visit often.

After replying to her mother, she still had seven more texts. All from a single person. Her ex. He was one of the reasons she'd jumped when Orson offered this job. She needed to get away, and yet, even here, he followed, if only electronically.

If Janine didn't have so many business contacts, she would change her number, but she refused to give in to his harassment. Although she did try blocking him. It didn't seem to stop him from finding a way to send her messages.

Message One: *Where are you? I went by your apartment and your car was gone.*

And it would be gone for a while, given she'd put her stuff into storage and was subletting the place. Given she didn't know how long her job with Derrick would take—she'd been exclusively hired to deal with him and him alone—she thought it best to get out. A part of her hoped Brian would give up while she was away, but in the meantime, he kept harassing.

Message Two: *Let's get together and talk. I miss you.*

Missed the prestige he thought dating a daughter of a council member would bring.

Message Three: *You didn't come home last night. Where are you?*

Ah yes, the stalking. Something she'd not told her stepdad or mom about, too embarrassed to admit the mess she'd made of her personal life.

Message Four: *You better not be fucking around on me.*

They were broken up. What she did was none of his business.

Message Five: *Why aren't you answering me?*

Because she never did. Answering would just open that door again.

Message Six: *You are a fucking whore.*

Only if the time she spent with her vibrator counted.

Message Seven: *Sorry about that last message. I miss you. I need you. Call me.*

Like hell. Sometimes, people assumed that someone in her profession, someone who dealt with people and emotions on a daily basis, would be smarter in their personal life. She was a psychologist. Shouldn't she know how to spot an asshat when she met one?

Nope. All her degrees didn't stop her from falling for a guy's sweet-talk, tight ass, and big blue eyes. She'd fallen in the trap so many women did. She fell in love with him, and that false love meant excusing some of Brian's behavior and allowing herself to get drawn into a pattern where he groomed her for future abuse, the verbal and controlling kind. She might have still been with him if he'd not slapped her.

At times, she thought she should send him a thank-you card for the physical reminder that this wasn't how a man treated a woman. The sting on her cheek had woken her up, and she dumped him.

Initially shocked, Brian didn't argue—other than calling her a moron for not realizing what a good catch he was. For a few weeks, everything seemed okay. Then the calls started, and, when she wouldn't answer them, the texts. When he'd dared to confront Janine coming out of her apartment building, she'd warned him to stay away or else.

"Or else what? You'll go to the cops?" He leaned in close, the whiskey on his breath strong. "You seem to forget, sweetcheeks, I own the cops. They work for me." At least that was Brian's view, given his role as district attorney and, since she didn't dare test it, possibly true.

Since a restraining order seemed out of the question, and telling her stepdad would see Brian meeting a hunting accident of some sort—probably mauled by an angry bear—Janine chose avoidance. Ironic, given she forced her clients to face their problems and fears, but a narcissistic individual like Brian fed off the drama and attention. She hoped by not giving him any, he'd bore of harassing her and move on to someone else. And, yes, she did feel a twinge of guilt and pity for whoever he set his sights on next.

"Why are you looking so serious?" He bobbed in the water in front of her, having paused his swimming to show curiosity.

She tucked her phone into her lap. "Nothing.

Just dealing with some email."

A crease furrowed his brow. "Do you always look annoyed when doing it?"

"I hate typing on small screens."

"Everyone does."

His hands braced on the side of the pool as he heaved himself out, slick, wet skin covering thick and defined muscle. She might have stared, she definitely gaped, and he turned his mighty glare on her, mistaking the reason why.

"Getting a good look at the crippled freak?"

She blurted out the truth, which, in this case, was totally inappropriate. "You have a great body."

Her statement made him recoil, enough that he lost his grip and fell back in the water with a splash.

Oh dear. She tossed her phone to the side and leaned forward, ready to offer him a hand. His fingers flailed from the water, linked with hers and…he yanked her in!

Chapter Five

On the list of things Derrick shouldn't do, dragging his new therapist into the water was probably one of them.

It's her own damned fault.

Telling him she liked the look of his body. A bald-faced lie. Had to be. What woman would find a man whose legs had lost so much muscle mass, and dangled limper than noodles, sexy?

What of the scars scoring his skin? Red lines. Bold spots. Jagged lightning leaving behind ridged skin. Most of his wounds had healed nicely, except for those drawn with silver. Those took much longer to heal, and they crisscrossed his body, telling a story that he couldn't forget.

And Janine saw them all. Saw all of his imperfections, didn't recoil from them, called him attractive, and then, to add even more insult, she offered him a helping hand.

She thinks I am weak.

Awoo. He almost howled with the indignity of it. Instead, he didn't think. He acted. More like yanked on the hand she dared extend.

She surfaced with a screech. "That's freakn' cold!"

Treading water beside her, he couldn't help but feel a faint tug on his lips. Surely not a smile? He clamped his teeth tight together. "It's refreshing."

"It's f-f-reezing," she managed to stutter through almost blue lips.

Hmmm, perhaps the little human was more fragile than he expected. Too bad. "Next time don't stare."

"How about next time you don't try and drown me?"

"You aren't in any danger." At this end of the pool, the water had a depth of just under five feet, and if she stood on tiptoe, she could keep her head above water.

"This is not how you are supposed to treat people," she chastised. "Especially not those trying to help you."

"Guess that was wildly inappropriate. Some would even say violent. I guess you'll have no choice but to ask for reassignment." Somewhere far away from him so he wouldn't have to fight the urge to lick her each time he saw her.

She slogged toward the shallow part of the pool and the stairs. Despite the chatter of her teeth, he heard her clearly. "You won't get rid of me that easily, wolf. Actually, I should thank you for this bonding experience."

He blinked. Tried to figure out her logic, but couldn't. "What the fuck are you talking about?" Perhaps the cold had affected her mental acuity?

"Part of building a rapport with your therapist is sharing experiences. Mind you, I think my teachers meant more of you sharing your past with me so we could work through it, but if you ask me, sharing a polar dip can also work. Just so long as you don't expect me to share my ice cream sundaes. Some things are best savored alone."

"Your logic is whacked."

"Maybe. And you're also not as crazy as you want people to think."

"I am too unbalanced." A weird retort and he might have said something else, except he almost lost his grip on the edge of the pool again. Her fault, of course.

He looked over as he hauled himself from the water to see she'd stripped off her blouse and wrung it out on the concrete patio. The sight of a woman in a bra shouldn't prove shocking. Tell that to his gaping mouth.

Managing a quick twist, he sat down hard on the edge of the pool, gaze riveted by the red-headed doctor, her skin a luminous alabaster in the almost midday sunlight.

Look away. Look the fuck away.

He didn't move a muscle.

Shirt wrung out, she laid it across the bench before stripping out of her slacks and giving them the same treatment.

Now, he would be the first to note that her bra and panties seemed of the very serviceable type, not even coming close to the skimpy bikinis he'd seen on beaches, but there was something about her standing in her undergarments, the intimacy of them, that made his mouth go dry.

His fingers twitched, aching to touch.

His watchful stare inhaled every nuance of her, sucking it in like a man starved. And in a sense, he was. When was the last time a woman disrobed in front of him?

Stop staring, you perv. He averted his gaze with the reminder that she didn't strip for his pleasure, but to get dry.

Speaking of dry, he reached around to the back of his chair and hauled out a towel. For a moment, he was tempted to be a selfish bastard.

Don't be nice. Don't show her any kindness. She has to leave.

Her frame shivered in the somewhat crisp air. Chivalry raised its not oft seen head. Sigh. "Heads up." He flung the balled fabric her way.

She caught it, not quite managing to hide her surprise. "Thank you." No gloating words. No triumph at making him do something nice. She simply toweled her damp skin and then handed it back.

He clutched the damp fabric, fabric that had touched her skin.

Don't be such a weird sap. He snapped out of it and dragged the towel briskly over his own flesh then folded it into a square and placed it beside him.

"You might want to look away now," he advised.

"Why?" she asked, only to then utter a very feminine, "Oh" as his fingers tugged at the waistband of his swim shorts. While he couldn't feel the damp fabric chafing his skin, he knew from past experience to change it lest his skin get irritated. Just because his dick didn't work wasn't a reason to let it rot off from an infection caused by neglect.

He tugged on his track pants quickly, the wheelchair at his back hiding his actions from those who might pass by. Bottom covered, he then grabbed hold of his chair and heaved his heavy ass back into the seat.

"You can look now," he advised. He reached

over to snag his shirt. He didn't put it on, though. He handed it to the doctor. "Put this on."

"Are you sure? I was going to toss my stuff back on."

Very sure because there was no way he was letting her walk back to the main building in sopping-wet clothes, and even less chance he'd let her roam about in only her bra and panties. "Wear it."

"Can I borrow the towel too?" she asked after donning the shirt. It covered her from neck to mid-thigh.

"Sure." He handed it over, and she wrapped it sarong-style around her hips, giving her an ankle-length terry skirt.

Scooping up her belongings, she slid her feet into her shoes. "Shall we go back to the residence? It will only take me a few minutes to run to my room to change so we can continue our session."

"I'm hungry." Not something he said often. The needs of his body didn't hold as much importance these days. However, that didn't mean he neglected his frame. Sustenance at regular intervals. Exercise too. He relied on certain basic structures daily to give him a purpose to keep going.

But how long can I use mealtimes and lifting weight to fill the emptiness in my life?

"We could have lunch together."

"No."

"Then we'll meet afterwards."

"I have physio after lunch."

Undaunted, she beamed. "Excellent. I will see you in the gym then. I'd like to meet your physical therapist."

"Why? If you read the reports, then you already know what he'll say. He'll tell you I've been a good boy who does his exercises."

She cast him a look. "I don't need to know what the report says. It's obvious from what I've seen so far that you've been working hard. Those kinds of muscles don't grow overnight."

She'd noticed? Sitting in a wheelchair didn't stop a man from pushing out his chest. "I've always been fit."

"And obviously motivated judging by your initiative this morning in going for a swim. You're doing great."

"If I'm doing so great, then why are you here?"

"Because rumor has it you want to hide it from the rest of the world. According to what I've heard, you refuse to see anybody other than the staff and patients here."

"I don't need visitors to come gawk at me."

"Your family wants to know how you're doing."

"Anyone who is interested can read one of my progress reports."

"Somehow I doubt knowing how many pushups and pullups you did and what you ate for breakfast is the same as knowing how you're really doing."

"I'm fine. That's all anyone needs to know."

"Don't your parents deserve more than that?"

That accusation slapped him, especially since he'd struggled with his choice to close himself off, but in the end, it was for the best. He stopped moving his chair, and she immediately noticed, her step halting. Spinning around, she fixed him with a quizzical stare.

"The guilt trip isn't going to work," he stated. She couldn't know he'd already argued with himself over this many, many nights. A part of him longed to pick up a phone and call his family, especially his mother. To talk to her and have that feeling she always managed to convey when he was a boy that everything would be all right.

But his mother couldn't fix things this time.

I'm truly and royally fucked. His mother would cry to see him so damaged. How could he bear to see the pity in his father's eyes for a son who was no longer a whole man? His brothers wouldn't know how to deal with him. They were all so healthy. What use would they have for a broken older sibling? As for his sister? Since she'd gotten involved with those dudes and had babies, Naomi had become a lot more girly. Still tough as nails and stubborn, but also emotional, and if there was one thing Derrick wouldn't tolerate, it was seeing his baby sister cry. *If she cries, then I might cry, then traumatize them all by wheeling my chair into traffic.*

Because, seriously, grown men shouldn't fucking cry. In public. Ever.

Best to stay away from them. All of them.

"You think I'm trying to guilt you into contacting them?" She shook her head. "Not if you're going to be a rude jerk. That wouldn't help you or them. No, when you do see them, it will be because you're ready to."

"That will never happen."

Never say never. He no sooner thought it than

she said it.

"Oh, it will happen. Eventually. We just need to get your head back in the right place again."

How about hidden between her thighs? Now there was a place he wouldn't mind visiting.

For a moment, he had a phantom recollection of an erection. The heightened awareness of his body, skin prickling as interest zipped across all his nerve endings. Then the thickening of his cock, inflating and awakening to show its appreciation. He could feel it. Wanted it. Wanted her…

For a moment, it felt so real. So fucking real! Alas, it was but a mirage. A fist in his lap showed the phantom erection as nothing but optimism, the flesh still soft. Dead.

And yet, the rest of him was not. The rest of him still tingled with that awareness. Even though his cock couldn't play, he wanted her.

I can't have her.

Never her, or anyone else.

Never to stroke the skin of a woman again.

Never to hear the soft sigh as her body arched from the pleasure he gave.

Never again would he bury himself in a warm, welcoming sheath. *Her sheath.*

Unable to look at her, or talk, because who the fuck knew what shit might pour out due to his suddenly pitifully whining, emasculated state, he took off, hands gripping the rims of the wheels, welcoming the hard bite as he grabbed and pulled and turned. A lot of exertion compared to the ease of motorized versions, but he didn't mind it. He preferred it. He needed an outlet when things got to be too much, and the constant exercise kept him strong. Strong enough to flee, but not fast enough to outrun his demons. Those found him, even in his dreams.

Chapter Six

Watching Derrick flee, Janine didn't give chase. Sometimes, a good therapist had to let a patient get angry. Anger was better than complacency, unless the anger turned destructive.

In Derrick's case, she didn't think he would harm himself or others. Not intentionally at least. His decision to avoid his family might seem selfish, on the surface at least, but she was trained to look past the words to the cause. *Derrick is afraid of hurting his family.* Not physically, but emotionally. Within close-knit families, if one person hurt, they all hurt.

Derrick understood his family would grieve his loss of mobility with him. Understood they'd do anything to make him feel as if nothing had changed. Would give up their lives to help him.

He didn't want them to do that.

Add to that the shame he felt, a shame that people could tell him he shouldn't feel but still did. You couldn't ask a man who'd spent thirty years of his life with vitality and an active lifestyle to suddenly accept restrictions. It would take time for him to swallow the bitter fact that one of the things he felt defined him as a man, his penis, no longer worked.

Impotence was a hard thing for anyone to accept. Some never did. All she could do, all anyone could do, was teach him that there were other things he could undertake to satisfy the urges he would still feel.

First, however, she had to get him to listen. Right now, his pride had him stubbornly shunning all help. Pride wouldn't stop her determination to get through to him.

The phone in her hand buzzed, and she glanced at it as she entered the building that offered rooms for the staff. Given the rehab center had patients twenty-four-seven and that specialists often flew in to give their expertise, a whole building, three stories in height, was dedicated to giving them a place to crash and call their own.

A quick press of her thumbprint and her screen lit up with a text message, which read: *Why aren't you answering my messages? You know I detest rudeness.*

The latest text to Janine from her ex, and par for the course since Brian detested many things. Most of them petty in the grand scheme, such as the fact that she liked a messy bed.

How Brian had freaked when she deliberately yanked the comforter down after he made it. Perhaps it was petty of her, but the same way he couldn't stand it looking messy, she couldn't stand a tidy bed. It made no sense to her. After all, why spread and tuck the sheets every day when they would just get ruined that same night?

She didn't have to look too far as to why she felt so strongly about it. She'd grown up in a home where beds *had* to be made. Father insisted. Father wanted the beds done tight and to perfection.

"If you can't bounce a quarter, then you didn't do it right."

Daddy didn't like slackers. He also didn't like himself after his last tour.

"What's wrong with Daddy?" she asked, the doll clutched under her arm. She couldn't get the stroller out of her closet because of her father. He crouched in there, arms around his knees, silently rocking.

"It's called PTSD. Something that happens to soldiers when they've seen bad things," her mother explained with an arm wrapped around her shoulders. She turned her away from Daddy that day, just like she turned her from the casket less than six months later.

But her daddy issues weren't why she dumped Brian and his military-made beds. The man was a control freak. *Where are you going? With who?* Followed later by, *Why didn't you answer my calls or texts?* Because after the third one in an hour asking when she was coming home got to be embarrassing. As for now, his constant texts acting as if they still dated were worrisome. She'd heard of guys having a hard time letting go, but this now bordered on ridiculous. She'd made herself clear weeks ago she wanted nothing to do with him, and yet, he still acted as if they were a couple, even showing up at the hospital she worked at the previous week, looking tanned from his business trip down south and expecting her to greet him with smiles.

"What are you doing here?"

"Is that any way to greet your boyfriend?"

Apparently, his escort out of the building by security hadn't hampered his delusion. He still kept calling and texting.

At least Brian didn't know where she currently was. She'd taken a three-month sabbatical from her regular position at her local hospital. She hoped it would be enough time to get Derrick on to a more even keel with the world and himself.

Such an angry man. Hurting and broken. A part of her wanted to wrap her arms around him, hold him, brush his hair back, and soothe him with kisses. Completely and utterly unacceptable. She was here to do a job, not do him.

It's unethical to even think it.

When she'd studied to become a therapist, she'd undertaken a certain oath, and part of that promise involved not taking advantage of emotionally vulnerable people. She was supposed to help them, not help herself.

The problem with being a psychologist was the annoying habit of diagnosing her own actions.

In getting suffering veterans to veer from suicide and self-harm, aren't I just, in fact, trying to atone for the reality I couldn't save my own daddy?

Funny how she told patients to not let their past govern their future, and yet, for her, it had decided her life path.

But I'm doing a good thing. Justification, the shield the righteous used to excuse their actions.

Having left Derrick to change, she took a moment to put in a call to her stepfather to report, yet it was her mother who answered. "June-bug, are you okay?"

She frowned. "Of course I am. Why wouldn't I be?"

"Your boyfriend, Brian, contacted us and—"

"He's not my boyfriend, Mom. We broke up awhile ago." Something she'd not divulged to her mother because sometimes keeping quiet just seemed easier than explaining she'd made a mistake.

"I guess that would explain why you stopped bringing him to dinner."

"You could say that." The fact that Brian brown-nosed her stepdad so hard they really should get a room also irritated her to no end. She preferred a man with a little more pride.

Like Derrick.

No, not like Derrick. He suffered from having too much pride.

"So I guess giving him the exact address where you're staying because he lost it and wanted to surprise you wasn't a good idea."

She sighed and closed her eyes as her fingers pinched the bridge of her nose. "No. It's all right. I can handle Brian. If he shows up, I'll just send him packing."

A few more reassurances were bandied about, as well as a promise not to miss their wedding anniversary party because her great aunt Fiona—who said for years Orson and her mom wouldn't make it—was showing and possibly about to change her mind. Mom wanted Janine to catch it on video.

Hanging up, she noted she'd arrived at her door. She tapped the card to get in and swiftly shut it, leaning against the portal with a sigh.

Despite what she'd told her mother, she wasn't unconcerned about Brian's possible appearance at the rehab center. With his credentials, they'd let him in. Why wouldn't they? He still looked like the captain of a football team—blond, tanned, and fit with a thousand-watt smile. A fierce mountain cat inside a suit and he wasn't afraid to use his claws.

She should have known better than to date a

shifter. They were possessive and territorial. Brian even more so than most. About a month or so after they began dating, she realized just how possessive he was. Meeting him in the lobby of her building for a date, she'd noticed him emerging from the alley, hand still tugging at his zipper.

"What were you doing?" she'd asked.

"Showing the world you're mine." As in marking his territory with urine. Romantic at the time, now pretty damned creepy. Funny how perspective changed things.

Enough, though, about Brian. She'd deal with him *if* he appeared. Big if. What kind of jilted guy chased a girl hours away?

A shower, a change of clothes, and a sandwich later, she went looking for her patient. She caught up to Derrick in the rehabilitation gym. He was lying on his back, the vinyl-covered bench supporting his body while he held over his head a heavily loaded barbell.

When her libido perked with interest at the bulging muscles and slightly sweaty body, she slammed her fist into her thigh.

No. She'd kicked her candy-bar-a-day habit. She could kick this craving for Derrick too.

The guy acting as spotter and trainer wasn't doing a very intense job. He sat straddling a second bench scrolling through his phone. Derrick pumped weight. Over and over. Without pause. Without strain.

The man was possibly part machine.

She came to a stop by his bench and frowned, first at the guy on his phone then at Derrick. "Shouldn't you be spotting Derrick in case he runs into trouble?" If he dropped that bar, he'd crush his chest.

The trainer peeked at her then Derrick. "You need help?"

"No."

"He's fine." And he went back to his phone.

She, on the other hand, was not fine and not about to leave it alone. This wasn't how things worked. "Aren't you supposed to be on him to work harder? To not give up? To, I don't know, make this challenging for him?"

"Are you accusing me of not doing my job?" Tucking the phone away, the other guy stood, and towered. She crossed her arms and stared right back. But the growling didn't come from her.

She tossed a startled glance at Derrick, whose eyes literally glowed with golden ire. The corner of his lip pulled back in a snarl, showing teeth, much more pointed than usual teeth.

Did the trainer know what Derrick was? She assumed he did, given the majority of the patients split their bodies with an animal. Yet, she knew humans worked here too. She couldn't tell if a man was shifter or not, and she knew nothing about this so-called trainer since she'd not read anything on the rehab center support staff, wanting to get a first impression as she met them before rendering judgment.

So far you're not getting a good grade, buddy.

"Ben, meet my new head shrink, Janine." Pump. The bar, laden with weights, rose and lowered. "She's young and idealistic and has all these grand ideas of how she's going to fix me."

"Only you can fix what's broken." She said

the words, and both guys laughed.

"Red, that is funny. Your optimism is cute, but so misplaced. Some things get too broken for repair. You have no idea what it's like to have seen what we've seen. To have endured. And, for some, live with the physical results daily."

"You might have suffered a fall and cracked like Humpty Dumpty, but you can glue some parts back together and go on."

"Did you just compare me to an egg?"

"She did," Ben snickered.

"It might not have been my best analogy, but the meaning is unchanged. You're broken, but that doesn't mean you can't pull the undamaged parts of yourself together and live a full life."

He rolled his eyes. "Fuck me, do you have to start with the feel-good shit already?" *Clang*. Derrick tucked the bar back onto the Y bracket. He pulled himself to a seated position and leaned forward, hands braced on his thighs. "If you're going to insist on following me around, then you need to do something more than blow happy rainbow smoke up my ass."

"Maybe I wouldn't feel a need to be so positive if you'd stop it with the woe-is-me shtick."

"You call these a shtick?" He slammed his legs with his fist. "I think I'm allowed to be a little pissed."

"Yup. And you are also allowed to be a dick, just like I'm allowed to tell you that you're being a dick."

"Doc, if I was a dick, you'd feel it." He leered at her, trying to sound and look ugly. Trying so hard to push her away.

"That's just crude. How would you like it if I made dirty jokes like that during a serious conversation?" She wasn't truly offended. Guys were sexual creatures, and some of them were more vocally expressive than others. However, given their doctor-patient relationship, she needed to establish a certain boundary.

Laughter startled them both as the trainer, who stopped skimming his phone again to chuckle at them. "Damn, you guys fight like a married couple."

"Out." Derrick pointed to the door. "I'm having a session with my therapist."

"That is the most fucked-up session I ever saw," muttered the trainer as he took his leave.

"And that's the guy they paired you with?"

"He's like the third one. The first two kept trying to tell me what to do. He lets me do my own thing."

"Why even schedule physio with a trainer at all if you're not going to use him?"

"It keeps the shrinks and other doctors from harassing me. They seem to think if I'm left alone to my own devices I'll turn into a lazy ass."

"I don't think you know the definition of lazy."

He gave an exaggerated sniff of the air. "I smell smoke."

"That wasn't a false compliment. You keep asking for the truth. I'm giving it to you. Sorry if it doesn't mesh with your perception of who you are."

"I know exactly who I am."

"A stubborn donkey."

"How is name calling suppose to cure me?"

he asked as he leaned forward to snag his wheelchair. She deliberately irritated him by grabbing it and parking it close to him.

Heave-ho. He made the transition with ease.

"It wasn't name calling, more like image association."

He cast her a glance. "Seriously? Is that what you're going with?"

A giggle left her. "Oh come on. That was funny."

"To who? I think you failed with the joke part."

"Have I? Later on, you'll think about me comparing you to a donkey and smile."

"No, I won't."

Having kept pace with Derrick's chair, she suddenly noted they'd traded the gym for the hall.

"Where are we going now?"

"I was going to take a shower."

"Do I need to call someone?"

"Nope. I'm a big boy."

"You're planning to shower by yourself?"

"Depends, are you offering to help?"

Yes! She almost said it. Almost slapped herself, too, for thinking it. "No, I'm not offering, just wondering. Your doctor's recommendation is you stay at the rehab center for additional support. Yet, from what I've seen, you seem pretty capable of taking care of yourself."

"Didn't do your homework? It's all in my file," he said, jabbing the elevator button that would take him down a floor to his level.

"I didn't want to taint my impressions. I'll read the entire file later, but for now, I want to get to know you, not some other person's summary."

"Well, if you had read it, then you'd know I have bad dreams."

"What kind of bad dreams?" she asked.

"The kind I wish I didn't wake from."

With those words, he exited the elevator toward his room, leaving her to stare after him, even after the doors closed.

At least he didn't try to avoid her after he'd showered and changed—without her help. Not avoiding, though, didn't mean they made progress. Their session that afternoon didn't prove very productive. Derrick wasn't in the mood to talk about what had happened to him overseas. Wouldn't open up about his family. Wouldn't talk about much other than the fact that he was fine and just wanted to be left alone. Normal behavior really for a guy like him who didn't want to let anyone get close.

Yet some of the tidbits he dropped, inadvertent ones, such as the fact that he had night terrors, sent her to bed that night to finally read his file and not just skim the basics.

It was hard to remain detached when she saw the pictures clipped within that showed his emaciated and abused frame when he'd been rescued. It truly sickened her to find out just how inhumane people could be. And for what? To claim a strip of land as their own? To say their God was better than another? Sharing and caring. Two simple concepts that, if adopted worldwide, would end so much of the strife and suffering.

Alas, nothing about the world was ever simple. Just like Derrick wasn't simple. A man of complexity, he would require careful handling.

Two hands, I'll bet.

Gasp. She blushed, even if she sat alone in her bed. How quickly and dirty her thoughts turned when thinking of the man. How utterly wrong. Here she read about how he'd survived something horrific and she couldn't help but see his bravery—and found him the more attractive for it.

A knock at the door startled her. "Who is it?" she called.

"Harold. The doctor on duty sent me to fetch you."

Opening the door, she noted the man dressed in blue scrubs with a receding hairline. "Where are you supposed to take me and why?" she questioned.

"We had a note left at the station saying if it happened again to let you know. Well, it's happening."

It involving Derrick, of course.

She grabbed a robe and followed the orderly as he led her through a basement level passage that linked the staff quarters and offices to the main rehab center. Entering the secured building, she noted the burly nighttime security guards flanking the doors and armed with Tasers. It made her think of a song by the Eagles. Something about checking in but forget about leaving.

The elevator waited for her, and she stepped in, only to notice the orderly didn't.

"Aren't you coming?"

He shook his head. "I've seen it before. And it's not pretty."

The elevator shuddered as it rose. The doors swooshed opened on her designated floor, and she immediately heard an eerie howl. Mournful, angry, and utterly uncanny. A shiver crossed her skin, raising the flesh in goose pimples.

Trepidation made her hesitate. What would she see? The file couldn't say what exactly happened at night just in case the humans got a hold of it. All the reports said was that the patient suffered from extreme night terrors. Of what, no one knew for sure. Derrick wouldn't talk about them. The prognosis? He relived some of the torture he experienced, a common side effect in trauma cases.

But why was there howling?

Upon stepping into Derrick's room, she noted a few things. First, his arms were bound to his bed, thick leather straps buckled around his wrists and secured with another buckle to the metal frame. Second item of note, Derrick's upper body heaved, arching high off the mattress while his head thrashed. Low, guttural sounds escaped him as his skin rippled. His eyes were shut, but she could see the rapid flutter of the orbs, a sure sign he was caught in the throes of a nightmare that he couldn't escape.

What worried her more, though, given the inhuman sounds rolling off his tongue, was the beast that thought it could burst free. If that happened, and someone saw, or worse, got hurt, even she might not be able to save him—or herself if she was in his path.

Chapter Seven

"Cripple." The word stung, even if flung by leering men with thick beards and cruel eyes. Derrick's captors taunted him with the fact that they didn't have to chain Derrick like the other prisoners. *Why chain the crippled man? It's not as if he can run away.*

How they liked to toss cruel barbs about his infirmity, their English broken and heavily accented. Yet the sneering jibes were easier to bear than the way they scored his body, dozens of small cuts, slices in his flesh, burn marks too, with wagers placed on how quick each one would heal. The fine lines didn't prove as painful as the yanking of his nails—one by fucking one. With guttural exclamations, they marveled when they realized they'd regrown by the next day. *Damn my ability to heal.*

The pain was almost more than he could bear. More than any sane person could handle. He'd thought the agony of shifting a torturous thing, and yet that proved fleeting compared to this daily abuse of his body.

Sometimes he partially let go, closing his human self and letting his feral side, beneath a thin human veneer of flesh, cope with the pain. It almost worked. Almost except for...

Why won't you let us change into our stronger shape? Let the wolf come out to play and tear into those that think to bring him low.

His beast side wanted to welcome the exulting agony of changing skin. Let the fur fly. Let the jagged teeth of his predator side snap and tear at those who thought to torture.

It's not allowed. The reminder faint and yet filled with will. *No. No. No.*

No matter the torture, the agony, everything they did, the one lesson taught from the crib was Derrick's mantra—"Don't let the humans know." And those who held him, despite their cruel torture, were most definitely human.

He had too much time to think in the darkness of his cell, too much time to count the seconds and the grains of sand in his cell, but he preferred the damp solitude to when they dragged him to that other chamber, and he meant dragged to then toss to the cold, dirty floor.

The dirt floor proved hard, and it didn't crumble, not with the blood tainting it and gluing the grit.

Before he could even think to push himself up on his arms, the lash whistled, the only precursor before it struck, a fiery line of agony across his back that stopped cold at his waist. The whipping, layered across not fully healed wounds, drew a gasp from him, nothing more because, with his throat dry and his cords raw, he had no voice left for screaming.

Whistle. Crack. Arch.

His fists clenched tight, and his eyes screwed shut. Animal instinct always took over when the pain became too intense. He pulled himself away, a strenuous drag with his hands and arms. Futile really because where did he expect to go?

Another flick of the whip. Slice. Another. He collapsed on the floor, not even caring his nose smashed first. So tired, so hurt, he could hardly move. But his captors were not done. They turned him over onto his back, the throbbing agony somewhat relieved by the pressure of the floor. Their raucous laughter and the whipping started again, this time marking his dead flesh, and while he couldn't feel the lashes on his legs, it proved a painful reminder that half his body was gone.

Gone.

Gone…

No. Sob.

Soft hands cradled his cheeks, and a soft angel voice murmured, "You're safe."

No one is safe.

"Wake for me, Derrick."

I want to. I want to wake from my nightmare.

"Don't make me dump cold water on your face."

I know that voice. Janine. She shouldn't be here.

The intrusion on his memories—relived nightly—snapped him awake. His eyes shot open, bleary as the brightness of his room and the darkness of his despair clashed. "What are you doing here? You shouldn't be here." Even with the cuffs he used each night, he could be dangerous. Mostly dangerous to himself—no big deal—but it was the others he worried about. They didn't deserve to suffer because he couldn't cope. *No one should get hurt because I'm too weak and broken.*

Instead of leaving, Janine clutched his cheeks and stared into his eyes, not with passion but intensity, the doctor in her checking his pupil dilation.

"They're glowing."

"The beast is strong at night."

"Strong enough to break free?" she asked, running her fingers along his jaw, such a personal embrace for a clinical observation.

"If my wolf were free, you'd know. I have a much more impressive snout than this. Bigger teeth too." He snapped his chompers at her when she tried to peer within. "Don't you dare. I'm not a horse."

"And you're not a wolf."

"Yet." Because how much longer could he keep his beast caged? It had been so long since his furry self ran on four feet.

The tips of her fingers pressed against his pulse, and he couldn't help staring at hers, a tiny flutter beneath tissue-thin skin.

A perfect spot to mark her.

He cast his gaze away, hoping she didn't note the sudden inhale of breath.

"Your heart is racing," she observed as she pulled away from him.

"It's the only thing that can anymore." The pessimistic words came so easily.

"Oh please. I saw the way you took off on me this morning. And I'll bet when you're pumping iron, no one can keep up."

"Petty things, and nothing like running the 400 meter or a steeplechase." The list of things he couldn't do stretched endlessly.

Her head tilted to the side. "I agree, it's not the same, so you need to redefine how you think of racing and realize it doesn't always involve two or four feet. Speaking of feet, when was the last time you let your wolf out?"

At the blunt question, his lips tightened. "You shouldn't be asking that."

"Why not? We're alone. I kicked out the orderlies, so it's just you and me. No secrets."

"In the spirit of no secrets, I feel like I should mention I sleep in the nude to avoid extra chafing." He couldn't help a wolfish leer, not with her so close, the soft scent of her calming his raging blood. She'd obviously come straight from bed, her chignon of red hair falling sloppily to the side, her robe, loosely belted over—

His head tilted as he squinted at the glimpse peeking through the vee of her sloppily belted dressing gown. "Is that a sasquatch onesie?"

"Bear actually." She opened the robe and flashed him the fuzzy brown pajamas. "Do you like it? My stepdad buys me one every year for Christmas. It's a bit of a dorky tradition we have. He gave me the first one when he adopted me."

"Dare I ask why?" Curiosity made him speak before he could bite his tongue.

"It started after I accidentally found out Orson was a bear. That Christmas, when we were done opening all our gifts, he handed me a present wrapped in polar bears wearing red bows. My mother knew nothing about it. He'd gone and gotten it on his own. Inside was a furry brown onesie. And do you know what he said to me when I pulled it out? That I would always be his cub." A hitch caught her words. "And it's true. He's been the best papa bear to me and my mom. As a reminder, every year, he gets me a new one."

"That is a ridiculously sappy story."

She smiled. "Yes. It is. But a good one."

The story raised a question, though. "What happened to your birth father?"

For a moment, he thought she wouldn't tell him. He could practically see her body shrink in on itself. Her gaze wouldn't meet his, and she pulled at a loose thread on her robe.

"Red?" He said her name in a soft query and almost wished he'd not asked, except now he needed to know. What could make this firecracker look so sad?

Her head lifted, and her piercing green gaze caught his. "This isn't how it's supposed to work. You're the one who's supposed to talk about your past, not me."

"That seems a bit one-sided. You want me to trust you with my secrets, but won't tell me yours?"

"My secrets have nothing to do with your treatment."

"Don't they? I have a feeling what you're hiding has everything to do with why you're here."

"You really want to know?"

"Yes."

"It's not a pretty or happy story." Her gaze finally met his. "My dad went through an experience similar to yours. He was in a tank that rolled over an IED. He lived, but the left side of his body was heavily damaged. He lost his leg below the knee and his arm."

"Your dad was crippled?"

She shot him a look, a dark, angry one. "He wasn't a cripple. They fitted him with a prosthetic so he could get around. Like you, they rehabilitated his body, but they didn't do such a good job on his mind. He went into a deep depression and killed himself. One bullet to the head." She said the words with a stark blankness to her features.

"Fuck." He'd suspected she had daddy abandonment issues, but never expected anything like that.

"I was only nine years old when he left me."

"I'm sorry." He didn't even try to stop the soft, comforting words.

But she wouldn't accept them. "Sorry for what? That my dad took the cowardly road and ended his life instead of learning to adapt? Sorry that he chose to die instead of staying with me and Mom?"

"That seems kind of harsh." He had to reply in the face of her vehemence. She didn't understand how hard it was to get up each day and live.

"Harsh is leaving me without my daddy. Harsh is making me believe I wasn't good enough to live for. What he did was selfish."

Even though he hadn't yet taken the step in the same direction as her father, he could see her implication. "I don't have any kids to miss me."

"No, just a huge family who calls daily to ask about you. Do you have any idea how lucky you are? Do you know how many people would trade spots with you in a second, as you are, simply to have a chance at that kind of love?" She stepped away from his bed, tugging her robe tight around her.

"Where are you going?" he asked, unable to reach out for her, the tethers he demanded nightly holding him prisoner.

"Back to bed. It's the middle of the night,

and I'm tired."

She's leaving? It made total sense.

So then why did he have the fiercest urge to say, *"Stay with me"*?

Sleep proved hard to achieve after her departure, his tumbles into slumber fraught with strange nightmares, and even some erotic ones. Cruel and taunting dreams where he was still a man able to seduce a woman. *Not just any woman. My woman. Janine.*

He woke from those shaking and sweating, yanking at the ties that bound him, his primal side lunging forth with the single-minded intent of tracking her down.

To do what? Claim her? Was he insane? Probably, given his experiences, and yet not insane enough to tether her to a broken veteran. Especially now that he knew why she'd chosen the medical profession. *In her mind, I'm her father. She wants to save me, not love me.*

Slap. The furry paw to his mental face snapped him out of pity mode. His beast refused to accept their limitations. Refused to let itself despair.

Around six-thirty in the morning, the orderly arrived to release him from his nighttime restraints. Freed, Derrick didn't immediately move, even when the sun rose and, with annoying precision, brilliant rays hit him full-on in the face. Usually, he grimaced and growled at the brightness. Today, he closed his eyes and let the warm rays dance upon his skin. He inhaled. Deep. And relaxed.

Despite the rough night, it surprised him to note no true signs of fatigue in his body. As a matter of fact, the sunlight bathing his skin felt nice. Very nice.

He didn't recall the last time he woke happy to see the sun rise. During his imprisonment, he recalled longing for a glimpse of blue skies instead of the daily darkness of his cell. Now, he usually dreaded it, as it meant a new day, a new reminder that not everything was right in his world.

Except, this morning, he didn't feel the usual dread. Instead, as he showered and dressed then ate, he found himself imbued with an odd sense of anticipation. He had a reason to rise today, a purpose, and much as he might deny the connection between him and Janine, he yearned for it.

Usually, he tried to avoid their ten a.m. meeting, but this morning, he found himself not trying to flee. Not that fleeing ever did any good. She always tracked him down.

Because I want to be found.

His wolf was the one to point that out because, in truth, if Derrick truly wanted to hide, she'd never find him.

However, this morning, he didn't lead her on a wild goose chase. He remained in his room, door open, waiting.

A few minutes after ten, he heard her light step outside in the hall then the prickling sensation that always touched him when she neared and let him know she'd entered his room.

She's here!

He whirled around in his chair, ridiculously eager to see her, only to freeze.

With a child nestled on each hip—looking oh so right—stood Janine. What the hell? Why did she have two ankle-biters with her?

The matching little faces were familiar to him. Very familiar. Panic crept into his body, tensing his muscles, gripping tightly to his lungs, making it hard to breathe.

"I brought you two visitors." Red jiggled the children.

For a moment, a dry mouth and a thick tongue wouldn't let him speak, and when he did, his voice emerged rough—big-bad-wolf gruff—especially once he realized who she held. "I told you no visits with family."

"You said no visits with family and friends who would look at you differently. Since the only time you apparently met these guys they weren't even crawling, I'd say they pass muster. I promise they won't judge or look at you funny."

They might not, but the fact that his niece and nephew were here, their chubby cheeks rosy, their eyes bright and inquisitive, meant their mother wasn't far behind. "Where's my sister?" He half expected her to pop out, even braced himself for the vibrancy of her presence.

Auburn locks bounced as Janine shook her head. "She's not here."

"She's not?" Surely he wasn't disappointed?

"You're not ready for that yet. But she is in town in case you change your mind. When I heard, I went to meet with her and asked to borrow these cuddly monkeys." She gave them a little squeeze and then took a turn nuzzling their cheeks, enough that they giggled.

As sounds went, it drove a dagger into his heart. Such sweet innocence. They shouldn't be allowed near him, not with all the darkness he harbored. What if it rubbed off? He didn't want to taint them.

"Would you like to hold them?" Janine stepped closer, and it wasn't just her scent that hit him—that brought all his cravings to the forefront—but the scent of baby powder and apples, a childhood staple that brought back memories of climbing the trees in his uncle's orchards when they visited his farm.

I can't climb trees anymore. Just like he couldn't be the uncle they needed. He recoiled from the idea of holding them, perhaps a little more violently than warranted.

She made a face at him. "You do know they're not contagious? Sticky, yes"—Janine smiled as she bussed his niece's cheek—"but they won't hurt you."

Their very presence hurt, an ache in his chest. *I survived the war to die of a heart attack.*

"You have to take them away before I hurt them."

"You won't hurt them."

How could she be so sure of that? Because he sure as hell didn't have the same conviction. "What if I drop one?"

A snort escaped her. "Since when do you lack the strength and agility to hold on to something?"

Should he be flattered she'd noticed his dexterity or annoyed she so easily poked a hole in his excuse? "I don't know what to do with kids."

"That's the beauty of children. You can just be yourself. They love without prejudice or conditions."

How dare she make it sound so tempting, within reach even. He closed his mind against the allure and fought back with words. "This is cruel. Bringing them here and reminding me of what I can't have."

"Says who?"

He shot a hot glare at her. "Have you forgotten about my problem?"

Her lips pursed. "First off, you can still have children. You're paralyzed, but your swimmers aren't. Having you own kids might require artificial insemination, but they would be one hundred percent yours. And second, how dare you accuse me of cruelty. It isn't cruel to remind you that you're not some monster who needs to be locked away from children. You're a man, a good man, and their uncle. So stop wallowing in your self-pity and start acting like one. Starting now. I need to pop downstairs and grab their diaper bag. Which means you need to watch them." She bent down so the children could slide from her hips to the floor, straightened, and walked away.

"You can't leave me alone with them. I don't know how to—" Except Janine wasn't listening or caring about his excuses as she exited the room, firmly shutting the door behind her.

She left me alone. Okay, not quite, there were two sets of curious eyes watching him from where she'd sat them on the floor. On the floor in reach of an electrical outlet. He remembered only too well what happened when his brother Stu licked one on a dare. He couldn't sit for a week.

The things that could happen brought a fluttery panic and his breathing quickened.

Calm down. Surely it wouldn't take her too long to grab their things and return. They could all just sit here until that happened. Sit and—

"Where are you going?" He couldn't help but ask, even if he wouldn't get a reply from his nephew, Mark, as the tyke took off on hands and knees with explorative intent.

The little boy checked out all aspects of the room, heaving and pulling at the blankets of the bed until he could clamber on top of the mattress. He didn't stay there long. He slid right off the other side, only to slither under the bed. He crawled out grinning and drooling before pushing himself to his feet and toddling, in search of more things to discover.

The girl, however, little Mellie, short for Melanie, sat and stared at him. Big blue eyes with superbly long lashes perused Derrick.

You're going to break hearts when you grow up.

And he'd break the faces of anyone who made her cry. It was his job as uncle.

A job I've been neglecting. Seeing his niece and nephew, seeing how big they'd grown and how much they'd changed from the pictures he'd seen reminded him of some of the things he'd missed out on. He couldn't blame it all on his service overseas. He'd chosen to shut himself off from his family.

It's for the best. What can a crippled uncle offer them?

He didn't need his wolf to slap him. Even he wanted to smack himself for such a woe-is-me thought.

Melanie leaned forward and placed her hands on the floor, using them to brace herself as she pushed out her bum and straightened her legs. She stood and grinned at him, the wide smile such an obvious look-at-me expression he couldn't help but be reminded of his sister, Naomi.

Little Mellie put her arms out for balance as she took wobbly steps toward him, and he held his breath as he watched, worried she would fall and anxious he wouldn't be in time to catch her. But she made it to him and cooed with excitement.

Even an ornery bastard like him couldn't help but smile. "You made it."

Made it to his legs and yet, she wasn't done. She leaned forward and grabbed a hold of his pants, and grinned at Derrick, the white protrusions of teeth adorable—and sharp, he'd bet. His sister used to have the same jagged maw. He remembered screaming more than once as a youngster when Naomi let him or one of the other brothers know of her displeasure.

But this sweet pup didn't nip him. She pulled at the fabric covering his legs, grunting as she tried to climb, her little feet not getting purchase. A scowl pulled at her lips, and she uttered an imperial, "Up."

Before Derrick knew what he'd do, he'd leaned over and scooped her onto his lap.

A happy giggle left her and she clapped her dimpled hands.

She should be proud. She'd just managed to get a grown man to do her bidding. The good news? No one was around to mock his weakness. Then again, was there any shame in doing this sweet child's bidding?

A hand, still slightly sticky with what smelled like apples and cinnamon, patted his cheek. "Dodo."

"As in dodo bird?" he muttered. He sure felt like an idiot.

The squeal by her brother drew Mellie's attention. She slithered off his lap like a pro and did an interesting crawl where her diapered butt stuck in the air. She disappeared behind the bed, and all Derrick could hear was happy cooing and alien baby language.

What had them so intrigued?

He didn't care.

"Ka. Or. Do. Ha. Ga." They kept conversing in twin language.

He drummed his fingers.

"Ooooh." The simultaneous sound finally had him pushing his chair around to see the twins playing with a pen they'd found on the floor. A pen that Mellie was using to write on her brother.

For a moment, he could only gape in horror at the blue squiggles on Mark's face. Then he laughed. And kept laughing because, dammit, he remembered doing the same damned thing as a child and his mother grumbling as she tried to scrub it from his siblings.

"Damn it, did you have to use permanent marker? We were supposed to get our family portraits done this afternoon." And they still had, the group picture owning a place of pride on the mantel, despite the fact that three of the children in it had black tribal markings on their faces.

The door to his room opened abruptly, startling the babies. Mark reacted by pushing to his feet and growling—which really wasn't all that impressive, given his gap-toothed grin and drool.

Mellie lunged at Derrick and squeaked, "Up.

Up. Dodo."

Since the princess demanded, he obeyed, scooping her into his lap.

With a diaper bag dangling from one hand, Janine stood in the open door, and her gaze immediately zeroed in on the baby in his lap. Worse, she smiled. Such an evil doctor.

He scowled at her obvious pleasure. "What is wrong with you, barging in like that? Never do that, not around my kind and especially not around a war vet. Some of us keep guns." He didn't because he feared the temptation of an easy out.

"Oops. Did I startle you? I didn't mean to do that." Total lie, he could see it, but why?

He narrowed his gaze. "What are you up to?"

"Are you accusing me of being devious?"

"Yes."

An unrepentant shrug lifted her shoulders as she stepped into the room and set the bag down. Mark abandoned his macho stance to go rummage in the bag. His sister joined him.

"Maybe I was sly," she admitted. "But only because you didn't leave me much of a choice. You're awfully stubborn."

"It's a family trait."

"So I've noticed."

"What I don't get is what you were trying to prove by leaving me with the kids. What were you thinking? I can't take care of babies."

"Why not?" Janine glanced at the two toddlers who'd located a bowl that had a flip-up lid and contained bite-sized cereal. "Looks like they did just fine."

"You weren't gone long."

"What exactly do you think would have happened if I'd left you longer?"

"What if they got hungry? Or, I don't know, started crying?"

"Given you are perfectly capable of feeding yourself, I don't know why you'd think they'd prove a problem. As to crying, what did your mother do when you were little and you cried?"

Being a man, he naturally lied. "Boys don't cry."

"Ha!" She snorted with evident derision. "Bull. Boys can and do cry. It's not a measure of your manliness if you do or not, just an indication that you can feel. Just like your legs aren't the absolute measure of your capabilities."

"Perhaps, but a lack of legs makes everything more difficult."

"I've already agreed with you that it does, but you need to realize that it doesn't mean you're incapable. For example, if one of the children had begun to cry, you would have been perfectly able to pick them up and soothe them, the same way you soothed Melanie when I entered abruptly."

As if the mention of her name was a sign, Mellie stuffed a last piece of cereal in her mouth and then monkey-walked back to Derrick. She didn't need to say a word this time, just lifted her arms and he picked her up. He wouldn't look at Red, though. "This is a cruel test."

"It's not a test but a reminder. You're still alive, and there are people who need you in their lives. Don't shut them out. Don't keep punishing yourself and them."

"I'm not punishing myself. I'm—"

"Don't you dare say it's for their own good. Because it's not." Green fire blazed from her eyes. "Stop being so damned selfish. You're not dead, so stop acting like you are."

Not dead. Funny how, a week ago, he might have disagreed. A week ago, he might have said the world would be better off if he was. But now...

Now, dammit, a part of me is eager to live.

Chapter Eight

Over the course of the next week, after the bombshell she hit him with by making him see his niece and nephew, Derrick seemed even more determined to thwart regular sessions. As if Janine would let his stubbornness get in the way of his treatment. She always managed to track him down and created opportunities on the go, but she couldn't have said if she was getting through to him.

For, as often as she got him to talk, in the end, he drew even more out of her with pointed questions about her childhood, asking about her life with her new father. How she worked her way through school so her parents could pay off the mortgage and have the security of a home for when the next financial crisis hit.

Surprisingly enough, despite their unorthodox sessions, she learned a bit about him, revelations that came spottily in between his outbursts, where he tried to push her away.

"Why do you give a damn?" he yelled one day when particularly annoyed. His wheelchair got stuck in a muddy rut, and she had to push him out. He didn't like that, didn't like dependence of any sort on anyone. "Why do you care what I'm thinking or what my plans are for the future?"

"I care because you're alive, and I want you to stay that way." Because, despite all their progress, a part of her feared he would go down the same dark path her father had. So many demons plagued Derrick, the biggest of all the one of doubt. He truly believed he no longer had a place or purpose in the world. That erroneous mindset had to go.

It was during the second week that she decided it was time, once again, to push him out of his comfort zone. Apart from the nightmares, Derrick appeared perfectly capable of getting around and caring for himself, but he'd grown too comfortable on the rehab grounds. Surrounded by the orderlies and doctors—who were, as he sneeringly put it, "Paid to be nice to the kooky patients"—and other wounded vets such as himself dealing with their own issues. Derrick needed a reminder that another world existed outside the gated confines of the rehab center. Of course, he initially refused to go.

Knowing he'd balk, she gave him very short notice. "We're going out tonight. In an hour actually. Somewhere off grounds."

"No, I'm not." His immediate reply.

"Think again. It's time you reintegrated with the real world."

"The real world can blow me."

The rude remark didn't even make her blink. "Not if you're hiding here, it can't."

He scowled. "Even if I agreed, I've seen your car. It's too small to take me and my chair."

She wouldn't ask how he knew what she drove. Chances were he'd investigated her. Curiosity, a healthy sign because it meant he was taking an interest in something other than his misery.

"You're right, my car is too small, but we're

not taking it. I got a special vehicle for tonight."

"Oh that sounds fun. I've always wanted to take the short bus," he griped.

"Stop being such a Debbie Downer. This will be fun."

"This is a bad idea," he growled just over an hour later as he wheeled himself out to the employee parking lot, his attempt to escape blocked because she guarded the elevator, expecting him to try.

"Everything is a bad idea to you. So stop bitching. It's very unattractive."

"Maybe I don't want to be attractive."

Did he know his lower lip jutted when he said it? "Too late for that. You're already cute."

"You think I'm cute?" Incredulity gave his query a high pitch.

At the realization of what she'd said aloud, she froze but didn't turn around. "Yes, you're good-looking, in a purely professional way, of course."

He snorted. "I am not going to sue you for sexual harassment. As if anybody would believe it anyway. Hot doctors don't lust after cripples."

The backhanded compliment warmed her heart, but his disparagement irritated her. She cuffed him in the head, not exactly an approved practice for therapy, but needed in this case.

"Hey! What was that for?" Derrick exclaimed.

"Being a dumbass. You are still a very attractive man. Being in a wheelchair hasn't changed that."

"Attractive doesn't mean I can perform."

"Is your sex education so woefully lacking? There is more to coitus than penile penetration."

Saying it out loud made her cheeks heat, and she could only hope he didn't notice.

A noise escaped him, half-chuckle, half-disbelief. "Wow, talk about sucking all the fun out of it. Penile penetration? Really?"

"Would you have preferred slamming the salami home?" Her rejoinder resulted in a rusty chuckle. "If we're done analyzing word choices, think fast." She twirled around and tossed a set of keys at him. His hand shot up and grabbed them mid-air.

"What are these for?"

"That." She pointed at the minivan behind her. "You're driving."

"Drive how? You know my feet don't work. Is this supposed to be another brutal reality check?" he snapped.

Pausing at the trunk, she replied, "As a matter of fact, it is. And you should have a little more faith. This van is a modified one. Gas and brake are by the steering column. Think you can handle that?" She arched a brow at him and leaned against the open cargo door.

"What if I don't want to drive?"

"Oh please, you've got too much testosterone to willingly let a woman drive you."

"Are you saying I'm chauvinistic? I'll have you know I have the greatest respect for women. I had to or my mother would have beaten me to within an inch of my life."

She grinned. "Not all chauvinism is bad. A little cockiness is what makes men, men. And one of the things men seem to enjoy doing is driving. So stop bitching and get your ass in the van." She pressed a button. "As you can see, it's got a ramp for your chair. I didn't get the van with the lift because I figured you could handle a little slope."

"It's a handicapped van?" He made a face.

"It's a modified vehicle adapted to those facing certain challenges."

"That's just a fancy way of saying handicapped."

"Maybe, and you're splitting hairs. Enough of that. I brought you something you could drive. The expected response would be, thank you, Janine, for being so thoughtful."

"Thank you for being a pain in my ass," he grumbled.

"You're welcome. Now get moving so we can hit the town. I think after the progress we've made these past weeks, we both deserve a drink."

"You're going to let me drink?"

"Why not? You've worked hard, and a drink or two won't hurt you." She could see she'd surprised him. He kept making assumptions about what he could and couldn't do. About how he could live. It was what happened when someone like him refused to listen and convinced himself he knew everything. Derrick needed someone to show him that he didn't.

"Once you're in the van, press this button to retract the ramp and this one to close the trunk." She pointed to the electronic controls. "Holler if you need help," she quipped as she stepped away from him. It actually took a lot of effort to walk away and let him deal with himself and his chair on his own. Manners said she should offer him a hand, and yet she knew he'd snap at any hand that dared to extend to give him help.

So, ignoring him, she clambered into the passenger seat of the van and pretended disinterest as the van dipped first when he hauled himself onto the bumper and interior lip. Then again when he dragged the chair in after him. He had, of course, eschewed the electric ramp extended from the van.

Whatever his method, he secured his wheelchair and made it through the wide gap between the seats, again a custom feature for this type of vehicle. He said not a word as he maneuvered into the driver seat. When he didn't immediately put the keys in and start the engine, she prodded him.

"What are you waiting for?" she asked.

"Still wondering if this is a good idea."

"If you really don't think you can't handle this, then we'll go inside. Maybe find a movie to watch. Or some crochet to pass the time."

Yes, she deliberately goaded him. He didn't want her to mollycoddle him, therefore she didn't, and she knew enough of his personality right now to know he needed the challenge to keep him motivated.

He jammed the key into the ignition and got the engine purring. "You're really sly," he observed as he squeezed the levers, revving the engine, and set the brakes.

"Just doing my job." Problem was the line between work and personal kept getting blurred. She already did and said too many things with Derrick that crossed ethical boundaries. She tried to relieve her guilt by reminding herself he wasn't like the human patients she dealt with day to day. Nor was he like the shifters she'd met via her stepdad. Derrick was so much more than any of them.

She must have spent a moment too long thinking because the van jolted, snapping her out of her fugue.

"Easy on the brake there. And to think people complain about woman drivers," she quipped.

"A little whiplash helps tone the neck muscles."

"My neck muscles are fine, thank you."

"Says you. But a woman should keep them fit."

The innuendo proved sly, but she caught it. "That was a very guy thing to say."

"Thank you. I'd like to think that even though the junk isn't working that I still am chauvinistic enough to maintain my standing in the man club."

"What is it with guys ascribing to misogynist attitudes?"

"Are you telling me you don't have the same kind of thoughts about dudes?" He shot her a glance, a rare teasing light in his gaze. "Oh, Marsha, you should have seen him with his shirt off," he mimed a high-pitched voice. "Think he can fix my car?" His voice dropped several octaves. "Have you seen the size of his feet?"

"That's another very guy statement. Why do you think women are obsessed with your size? We're not, you know. When I date a man, I don't think about his, er, girth." Yeah, she stumbled a little and blushed. "Compatibility and an ability to stand each other when not being intimate is more important."

"Are you denying that sexual intimacy is a huge factor?" He sounded angry, and she knew he expected her to say sex didn't matter. She wouldn't lie to him.

"Intimacy is very important in any relationship, but there are many ways to achieve that intimacy. As I said before, not all of them require penile penetration." She stared at the hands in her lap, trying to maintain a professional composure, and failing miserably. Heat suffused her.

"You keep saying I don't need a dick to fuck and keep a woman happy. So what do I get out of it?"

"Have you never sexually pleasured a partner just because it would be enjoyable?"

"Yes, but it was different."

"How was it different? Didn't you enjoy it?"

"Yes, I fucking enjoyed it. But I also knew I could fuck her if I had to. Now, all I've got is my tongue and fingers. Nothing else."

"I wouldn't say you have nothing. Even you admit there are other methods."

"Is this your way of telling me to get my tongue in shape? Maybe get my hands manicured so they're soft for finger-fucking? How about a strap-on so she can get the feel of a hard cock slamming into her?" As they ventured into uncomfortable territory, he resorted to crass words.

She could handle crass. It was the vulnerability that drowned her. "I'm not going to explain the various methods you can use to achieve satisfaction because you obviously have a good idea. But I am going to address the fact that I think you're afraid you'll get nothing from the experience. And I won't lie and tell you it will be the same. It won't. Yet, while you might not ejaculate in the regular sense, if you allow yourself, then you can still achieve a certain amount of pleasure from the act. You can find sexual fulfillment."

"Are you seriously going to try and convince me that I'm going to have some kind of phantasm orgasm?" He uttered a derisive snort. "Maybe I'll shoot some ectoplasmic cum."

"Why are you so scared to believe me?"

She noted his knuckles turned white where he gripped the steering wheel. "I'm not afraid."

"You're lying, and I don't know why. Haven't you figured it out yet? We're all afraid, Derrick. Every single one of us faces fear on a daily basis. Life is a series of challenges. It's up to us to meet them head-on."

"And what if we fail those challenges?"

"Then, you try again. Don't be a quitter." At those words, he turned silent. She broke it as they neared their destination. "Turn here. This is where we're going."

A rapid twist of the wheel brought them into the lot, and he quickly parked. As she stepped from the van onto the gravel, she could hear the retro metal tunes blasting from the bar. She made her way to the back and opened the trunk, only to realize Derrick still sat in the driver's seat.

"Aren't you coming?" she asked.

"I don't know if I can do this." The soft admission probably didn't come easy. She clambered in through the back and made her way to a spot behind his seat.

"If you really think this is too much or too

soon, then we'll leave." She reached through the seats and gripped his hand. "But I don't just think you can do this, I know you can. It's time to face the world again, Derrick."

"By hitting a bar?"

"You have to start somewhere. Would you prefer another place?"

For a moment he sat, not replying. He sighed. "I really hate your subtle bossy nature."

"Then let me try and not be subtle. Get your ass out of that seat. I'm thirsty, and you're buying the first round."

"I am?"

"Yup."

Given his eschewing of the ramp before, she jumped out of the back, grabbed his wheelchair—staggered a bit as it took her off balance—and set it on the pavement. Then she struggled a few minutes to open the damned thing. When she looked up, she noted Derrick sitting on the bumper, shaking his head.

She gestured to it. "Your chariot awaits."

"You do know I could have done that in half the time?"

"A thank you would suffice."

"A thank you will depend on my rage levels once this new experiment of yours fails."

"Have a little faith." Hopefully, he didn't notice the fingers crossed behind her back. This part of the rehabilitation plan required other people, strangers. She just hoped she got a good bunch, or she might set him back. Derrick sat at an apex in his treatment right now. It required careful maneuvering lest she send him tumbling down the wrong side.

As they approached the bar, the music getting louder, she began to second-guess herself.

Is he ready for this? Maybe we should go somewhere quieter, just the two of us. Yeah, because what she needed was alone time with Derrick.

Avoiding intimate scenarios was the exact reason she'd brought him to such a public place. More and more she found herself drawn to this man torn by his past and emotions. She discovered a vested interest in his well-being and future, an interest that wasn't professional. This was about more than making sure he didn't follow the same path as her father. This was about more than accomplishing a job.

I want him to succeed. Because then he wouldn't need her as a doctor, and if he wasn't her patient...

Just thinking of something more should have sent her back to the rehab center and making a phone call to her stepdad to be replaced. Instead of doing the right thing, though, she followed her heart, right into the bar with Derrick.

Chapter Nine

What the fuck am I doing here? Derrick hadn't set foot—or wheel—in a bar since his accident. Bars served alcohol, which he tolerated better than a human, but drink enough of it and his inhibitions lowered just as much as the next guy's. Lowered inhibitions, though, meant his wolf, the wolf who wouldn't stop pacing, pushing to take over. His wolf loomed within, so much stronger now, strong enough that Derrick worried.

Oddly enough, getting drunk and going loup on a room full of people wasn't his biggest concern. He could handle his wolf. What Derrick didn't want was to be stared at by able-bodied guys. He didn't want to see the pity in their eyes, the disdain for the cripple.

Am I truly condemning them without giving them a chance?

Never mind he'd never shown that kind of attitude to people he'd known with infirmities. Although he'd never done it, Derrick had seen it. Hated it. Used to punch those who disparaged the less able bodied. In some cases, he made them apologize—*Remember Timmy Reed?* He'd lost a leg and his parents in a car accident in grade nine. Timmy went on to do great things, but Derrick never forgot how those boys in school treated him. Pummeling him with words, and Timmy, never defending himself. Not even bothering with words because, as he told Derrick later, "Some people just don't know how to listen or see past the surface. They don't see that I'm still me inside."

Derrick didn't think he would handle that kind of disparaging attitude as well as Timmy had. He wanted to be seen as more than "that poor man stuck in a wheelchair." He doubted he'd stay quiet if someone dared mock him.

Bite their face off. His wolf wouldn't tolerate disdain—even if deserved.

Wheeling into the place, the stairs flanked by a ramp—that he assumed was put in for deliveries because his mind refused to see—they entered the bar, Janine holding the door open for him. The stupid reversal of roles put a scowl on his face.

Mama always taught me the man holds it open for a lady.

Did doctors count too? He kept trying to remind himself she was off limits. But Janine made it hard—not in a cock-teasing way, unfortunately—to think of her platonically. Just a glimpse of her, the barest whiff of her scent, and every atom in his being blossomed with awareness. Every atom above the belt that was.

Even their talk in the van about sex—and the fact that he couldn't have any!—did nothing to stir any interest from his limp snake. She could claim all she wanted that a man could satisfy a woman in other ways, and yes, she was technically right, they could. Derrick wasn't stupid. He knew how to make a woman come without his rod, but he wanted more than simply a taste and touch. *I want to be able to sink into her. To feel her clenching around me. To feel the quiver of her orgasm.* How could he ever properly claim a woman—not just any woman, Janine—if he couldn't slide his cock into her and brand her with his flesh?

There are toys.

Toys were made of plastic. A woman deserved more. A mate deserved a whole man, not a half one like him.

And here he was still thinking of her in mating terms. Janine surely thought him pathetic the way he drooled after her like some lovesick pup.

Dislikes me so much, she dragged me to a bar. A more pathetic guy would have read something into that, maybe a reciprocal interest. Pragmatism was for those who could walk. Derrick knew this outing was nothing more than another step in his treatment plan.

She's here to fix me. What a waste of time.

"Why are you scowling so badly?" she asked as she sat down at a two-person table. She didn't remove the seat across from her, so he did it himself, dragging the wooden chair to the side to give himself a spot to park. She didn't offer to help at all. He hated it when she respected him that way.

How dare she keep proving I can take care of myself! Surely some kind of crime deserving of punishment?

Like a kiss.

No kiss.

Grope?

Apparently, his dirty mind was in fine form this evening and he'd not even downed a single drink yet. He drummed his fingers on the table. "I'm scowling because this was a bad idea. Everybody is staring at me."

"No one is staring," she replied, peeking at the laminated menu of drinks. "And if they are looking in our direction, they're probably staring at me. In case you hadn't noticed, I'm the only woman in the place other than the waitresses. They're probably wondering if I'm available."

"You're with me," he growled.

"As your doctor," she reminded.

"But they don't know that. They shouldn't be staring." He aimed his glower at the room in general.

A glance around showed that, while a few stray glances were tossed their way, she was right. For the most part, they just slid over Derrick without expression and lingered over her, with a little too much interest.

Rip their eyes out. Tear at their throats. How dare they sniff around our female.

He blinked at the strong surge of emotion from his wolf. What made it more uncanny? He felt the same jealousy—minus the whole ripping and tearing thing.

Staring down at the table, he drew deep breaths, trying to calm his inner beast and panic. She mistook his agitation.

"Is this too much for you? I didn't think it would be this packed with people. We can leave if you'd like."

Leave and admit his cowardice? Never. He angled his chin, stubborn to the core. "I'm just peachy fucking keen, Red. No worries here."

A young blonde sauntered their way, her hair swept into a ponytail, her jean shorts tight and borderline indecent. The blouse she wore sported a checkered pattern and was tied off around her midriff, under pert breasts pushed high by her bra.

Cute, but not his type. He preferred the woman across from him.

After a perky hello and a quickly rendered listing of their on-tap specials, the waitress took their order, her smile bright and cheerful and her gaze not once lingering to his chair. She treated him as if he were normal.

But I'm not!

He never had been, even before the accident, but the wolf he could hide. This he couldn't. No one could miss the fact that he sat in a wheelchair, that his legs did not bear a cast. All could see his shame, and yet, no one remarked on it. He strained through the music, waiting to hear a disparaging remark. Either the music muffled it or no nasty rejoinders were made.

Kind of disappointing really.

The food arrived, a basket of crispy fried onion rings and coconut-covered shrimp. Tastiest shit he'd eaten since he'd gotten home. So tasty he ordered some wings and fries, delighting in their flavor, so much better than the bland rehab center diet.

"Someone missed junk food," she said with a laugh as he polished off the last wing.

"I don't remember the last time I ate this much," he admitted.

"Nice to see there are things that whet your appetite."

"If you wanted me to eat, then we should have smoked a joint."

She shook her head. "There you go trying to shock me again. Nice try, and just so you know, I've used marijuana in some treatment plans to deal with a lack of interest in food."

"You've intentionally given your patients the munchies?" He gaped at her.

"Don't act so shocked. It's proven to be an effective drug in many treatments."

"I'm not shocked. Okay, I am, but mostly because I thought doctors all had this huge bias against it."

"Not all doctors. When it comes to treating people, there is no one fit. Everyone is an individual, and I find the best results when I follow my instinct instead of the standard rules."

A deep conversation to have, and yet, as usual, when talking with her, he found himself responding to her easy manner. She disarmed him with honesty and earnestness. She surprised him constantly, like with his discovery she loved football, and wouldn't you know it, they rooted for rival teams.

She enjoyed caramel on her sundae and honey in her coffee. Whereas, he liked chocolate and took his black. Yet for their differences, they found common ground, such as their love of fishing, and closet addictions to *Dr. Who* and Burger King Whoppers.

The mundaneness of some of their discussions almost proved surreal—and pleasant.

"What is this accomplishing?" he asked, interrupting her interpretation of the current Western song crooning about a woman who'd left.

"Well, according to the guy singing, he should have taken the trash out instead of sleeping with it."

"Not the whole cheating thing, I mean this. Bringing me here. I already knew I could leave the rehab center grounds and go out. I chose not to."

"Which is why I made you. Time to stop avoiding the real world."

"Maybe the real world is better off without me."

"Don't say that. Don't ever say that." She grabbed at his hand, the move so sudden, so electric he could only dumbly stare at the conjoined fingers. His tanned, callused skin against her softer white hands. "You can't give up."

"I never said I'd give up." That was the height of cowardice to him. "But one day, I might lose the fight."

"You'd better not be talking about killing yourself." A tremble of fear heightened her tone.

"I'm not."

"Then what do you mean?" She'd no sooner queried than her eyes widened. "Are you talking about your *wolf*?" She leaned in and whispered the word. "Are you having problems with control during the daytime too?"

The dilemma—to admit or not to admit his wolf fought him twenty-four-seven. "If I told you I am in a constant battle, what would you say?"

A line of worry streaked across her brow. "I would say you have to get it under control. And I mean that most seriously."

"Or else what?" Because she seemed quite frantic.

She bowed her head. "Or you will quietly disappear."

For a moment, he said nothing, stunned by

her words and wondering if he misunderstood. "What do you mean by disappear? Will you have me locked away?"

"No. You wouldn't get a cell. You should know the council prefers a more permanent solution to feral situations."

The implication slapped him, and he snapped back in his chair. Had she seriously said they'd kill him? She'd know, wouldn't she? After all, they'd sent her to deal with him. "They want to kill me."

"No they don't, or I wouldn't be here. They want you to get better."

"And if I don't, then I die." The irony didn't escape him. He might have survived his ordeal overseas, but the nightmares might be what got him killed. He leaned forward and hissed. "Is it you who will pull the trigger?"

"Of course not," she snapped. Fiery green eyes fixed him. "I am here to help you, not kill you."

"Help me or make sure the big bad wolf's not going to start eating the humans?" The realization she held his life in her hands bothered him.

"I never hid the fact that the council sent me."

"No, but you did hide the fact you're supposed to fix me or they'll put me down like a rabid dog." He drummed his fingers on the tabletop. "Can't say as I'd blame them. We can't afford our secret coming out. So how long do I have to reform my ways before a hunter is sent?"

"You're not getting killed." Said with such vehemence. Perhaps she did care.

Caring wouldn't stop a judgment against him.

"You won't be able to stop it if the council orders it."

"They won't order it because you're going to get better." She slammed her hands on the table, her expression bearing such passionate conviction. "So stop fighting me on everything."

"But I enjoy fighting with you." Especially when heat brightened her cheeks and flashed in her eyes.

"That is such a guy thing to say." She pushed her chair away from the table and stood. "I'm going to the bathroom."

He couldn't resist teasing her some more. "Do you really need to pee or are you going to call and put in a status report?"

"Pee. I have a gerbil-sized bladder, and that drink went right through me." With a toss of her red hair—as fiery as her spirit—she sauntered off, pert ass swinging in hip-hugging jeans.

Way too many gazes followed her path. A small growl rumbled from him.

Don't let them touch her. The possessiveness made him curl his fingers around the frosted glass bottle of his beer. Just the one drink, and only half sipped. He wasn't taking chances with his wolf. He could handle the alcohol just fine so long as he didn't overindulge too quickly.

A shadow fell over him, but Derrick knew the human approached when he was still a few feet away. Very few people could hope to sneak up on a shifter. Derrick didn't bother looking at the human. He could smell him—sweat, leather, and men's cologne. Sniff. A hint of diesel mixed in there too. Probably a truck driver popping in for a brew after work. Or a construction worker. Whoever the man was, he'd invaded Derrick's personal space.

"What do you want?" he snarled while his wolf paced with great agitation.

"I want to buy you a drink."

Chapter Ten

Upon returning from the washroom, where Janine emptied her pitifully small bladder and spent a moment pep-talking herself in the mirror—*don't lust after the patient, stay professional*—she returned to find Derrick surrounded by burly bodies…and they were all sharing a bottle of tequila?

She blinked, but the scene remained the same. What happened while she was gone? Whatever the reason, she liked it, given these men gave something Derrick needed. Acceptance.

It was one thing for her to preach he could live a normal life, another for people to treat him normally, to tease him and swap scar stories.

She did her best to remain unobtrusive, sliding into a chair alongside Derrick, yet he knew she was there. To her surprise, he reached out and grasped her hand, and kept holding it the rest of the evening.

She'd never seen him more relaxed, so she was surprised when he announced, "Time for me and Red here to go."

Despite the many shots and the beer he'd polished off, Derrick could still wheel himself out of the bar, but a good thing he sat in a chair because he was definitely tipsy, as his path veered from left to right. As they neared the van, she held out her hand. "Give me the keys. I'm driving."

She expected argument. Men ever did have a problem admitting they'd drunk too much. To her surprise, Derrick pulled the keys out and handed them to her, the metal still warm from the closeness of his body.

"Let's see how you handle those wheels, Red."

The regular use of his nickname for her should have prompted a reminder of her title, Dr. Whelan. She didn't correct him, as she couldn't help a certain guilty pleasure at his appellation.

He didn't argue about the ramp she lowered to help him board. Nor did he comment when she gave him a push to align him correctly lest he tip off. He managed to belt himself into the passenger seat and then proved himself a loquacious drunk.

"I will probably deny it in the morning, but I enjoyed going to that bar."

"You might deny, but you'll remember," she stated with assurance as she guided the vehicle onto the dark road only occasionally lit by other cars' headlamps.

"I shouldn't have drunk that much. It makes my wolf harder to hold at bay," he confided. "The things it wants to do…" He trailed off.

"What things?"

"You shouldn't ask. You don't want to know."

Did he worry that the violence of his other side would turn her off? She'd already learned to adjust her thinking when it came to dealing with shifters. Their worldview tended to be a lot less forgiving and a lot more physical than some humans could handle. All part of sharing their psyche with a wild creature. "Tell me. You can tell me anything."

"But aren't you the one constantly reminding me you're my doctor? Did you know I keep trying to remind myself too? I keep trying, but my wolf…" He shook his head. "My wolf, it wants to eat you all up."

The van swerved as she managed a not quite calm, "It wants to kill me!"

"Not kill." He chuckled. "I mean *eat* as in get between those sweet thighs of yours and lick my way to nirvana."

A part of her understood the alcohol spoke, yet it didn't stop the quiver between her legs. She clamped them tight. "You shouldn't be thinking those kinds of things about me, although I am very happy that you're at least starting to think of sex in a positive way."

Clothing rustled and the springs on his seat squeaked as he turned to face her more easily. "More than think. Want. I can't help but want the forbidden fruit. I can't stop thinking about and craving it."

"You know we can't." Even if she desired the same thing.

"You're right. We shouldn't."

"We have to keep our relationship professional."

"Absolutely."

They totally agreed, so why was it the moment she slid the van into the parking spot that they both unlatched their seatbelts and came at each other?

Their lips met in a clash of teeth, his hand threaded through her hair to cup her head and draw her close. Her fingers curled at his shoulders, squeezing the tense muscles.

A part of her knew how wrong this was. So very, utterly wrong. It didn't stop her hot, panting breath, the sensuous slide of her lips on his, the sucking and gnawing of tongue.

Hunger unleashed in her, a hunger matched by his passion as their lips embraced and their hands stroked what they could through clothing. Every part of her hummed, alive at this sensuous—

Knock. Knock.

The abrupt interruption had her dragging herself away, lips swollen, heart racing, and desire unquenched. For his part, Derrick appeared just as wildly affected, his eyes partially shuttered with desire. A desire they had to ignore, no matter what their bodies craved.

Who knew what might have happened if not for the knock on the driver side window and the shine of a flashlight?

With the engine off, the electronic window wouldn't roll down. She cracked open the door and blinked at the bright light directed her way.

"Everything all right, ma'am?"

"Fine. Just fine. Just having a chat with my passenger before going in." A chat that involved lips, but not much in the way of words.

"Who's your passenger?" The light angled over her shoulder as the security guard leaned forward to peek.

She caught the animal sheen in Derrick's eyes and knew the guard did too. His hand dropped to his waist. He didn't have a gun, none of the guards allowed near the patients did; however, he did have a walkie-talkie, which meant access to guards with weapons. *And I'll bet if he works here, they know what they're dealing with.* Which means they'd shoot rather than risk a feral getting loose.

A low growl rumbled from inside the van.

"Get out of the van and move out of the way, ma'am."

She slid her feet to the ground, but remained firmly planted in the door.

"He's not dangerous. I promise. You have nothing to worry about."

"He just growled at me," the guard replied, his own eyes taking on a primal cast she'd come to recognize. The guard was a shifter.

"Give him a break. He had a few beers and was making out with me," she boldly stated. "And you interrupted. He's a little peeved right now. Wouldn't you be?" The truth would serve her in this case—even if it bit her later as proof she should excuse herself from this case.

"Making out in a parking lot?" The guard shook his head. "Aren't you two too old for that kind of shit? Get a bed."

"We will," she promised.

"We will?" Derrick mimed in a high-pitched voice once the steps for the guard faded into the darkness of the parking lot. "We will smack him for being a cock-blocking dickwad who should know better than to come a-knocking when the springs are a rocking."

"We shouldn't have been doing that," she retorted as she opened the back of the van. Derrick moved quickly, and he was the one to toss down his wheelchair. She caught it before it tipped over.

"Of course we shouldn't be making out." The words emerged flat. "For a moment, you forgot what I was. Just like I almost forgot. I guess I can't accuse the guy of cock blocking. We both know it wouldn't have gotten that far."

"It would have gone far enough," she muttered. She took a few paces before she noted Derrick didn't follow. Janine turned around and saw him sitting in his wheelchair, his face a study in agony that quickly hardened.

"Why do you insist on torturing me like this?" It didn't emerge as a plea. Anger radiated from him, and a wild shine entered his gaze. "Haven't I suffered enough? Do you have to remind me daily of what I can't have? But want. Crave with a hunger you cannot imagine and yet must starve myself."

"Lust is a healthy thing. There are lots of women—"

"Not women. One woman. You don't understand the agony you're putting me through."

"I'm not doing it on purpose."

"Perhaps not. Just like I'm not desiring you on purpose. But I can't help myself. My wolf says you're my mate."

"That can't be." A negative shake of her head didn't erase the words between them.

"I couldn't agree more. We all know I can never be a real mate to anyone."

"Don't twist my words. You know that's not how I meant it. We need to keep things professional."

"Oh, don't start with the excuses. I really don't give a rat's ass I'm your patient. I will tell you right now, Red, if it weren't for this"—he slammed his fists onto his legs—"I would claim you. I would grab you by that silky hair and pull you in to me. I'd bite that neck of yours and mark you for the world to see as I enter you from behind. I would fuck you until the only name you'd remember is mine."

A sharp breath sucked in. Heat pooled in her lower body, liquid heat that sent a tremble to her legs.

"Here's the thing, though, Red." Derrick wheeled closer, his stare never relinquishing her from its grip. "It doesn't matter if you're my mate because I can't do it. Can't. Fucking. Do. It." Said so softly, almost deadly. "And that fact is slowly driving my wolf mad."

"I can't be your mate. You must be mistaken."

A snort left him, derisive and abrupt. "No mistake. But don't worry. I won't saddle you with a cripple."

"You're not—"

"Don't start. Don't say another word. And run. Don't look back."

"I—"

"I said fucking run!" He barked the words at her, and something in his tone made her spin. She knew it was the wrong thing to do, not because she let a patient control the situation, but more because she feared the wolf.

Derrick himself said the wolf pushed to dominate. The wolf pushed its agenda and needs onto Derrick. The wolf was taking over. The signs were all there, and yet when she answered her phone about ten minutes or so after she made it to her room, skin flushed and panting, she wasn't ready to admit defeat with Derrick.

The first thing her stepdad said was, "Are you all right?"

"Of course I'm fine. Why wouldn't I be fine?" She kicked off her shoes and padded into the washroom, the only place with a mirror. She stared at her still-kiss-swollen lips.

"I just got off the phone with a certain patient of yours."

"Derrick called you?"

"Which is the first thing wrong. How the hell did he get his hands on a phone?"

Not as hard as her dad thought. She'd seen many patients with one. Derrick could have easily borrowed one, but how did he know what number to call?

"What did he want?" she asked. For a mentally deficient moment, she actually wondered if he'd called her dad to ask permission to court her, olden style.

"He wants you off his case. Says he's fine and just needs to be alone."

"He does not need to be alone. He's just saying that because he's mad at me." *Mad because he wants to make love to me.*

"And him being mad at you is part of your reassuring speech?" her stepdad queried. "What is going on, June-bug? Why is Derrick calling me? Who the hell even gave him my number?"

She'd guess he either acquired it via some hacking in the main office or quite simply swiped her phone at one point and trolled it for numbers.

Sly. Slick. Devious. Excellent. Forget apathy.

His mistaken belief she was his mate pulled him from his fugue.

Are you sure he's mistaken? What if she truly was his mate? She'd certainly heard of it. Orson claimed it with Janine's mother. Said he knew from the moment they met she belonged to him. As for her mom, she giggled and blushed.

So enviable and yet impossible, especially with Derrick.

"June-bug? What is wrong? Actually, I know what is wrong. I should have never sent you there. I knew the man was borderline feral. All the signs are there."

"He's not feral, Dad. And I'm going to prove it to you. Just give me a few days. You'll see."

As soon as she hung up, she immediately wondered how she could prove Derrick wasn't dangerous. Only one idea came to mind, and she stalked over to his dorm to tell him the next morning.

Bright and early. Too early, apparently.

Chapter Eleven

Red stalked into his room, swinging the door open in a familiarity that apparently didn't see a need to knock. "Derrick, we need to—Uh. Oh." Her outburst ended on a gasp. Probably because she got more of a glimpse than she expected

Splayed on top of covers still drawn tight, one hundred percent naked, and bound—the height of emasculation—he glared. "Were you raised in a barn?" Something his mother used to accuse him of when he lacked manners. His Aunt Joni took great offense at that expression and claimed it was those raised as ci-diots that were the problem with morality nowadays. A shame they feuded for years on end. Aunt Joni's pie was worth the occasional brawl between sisters.

Janine's head ducked. He could only imagine the pinkness of her expressive cheeks. "Sorry. I didn't think. I'll come back later when you're not so, um, er, tied up," she stammered.

The things she could do to me right now…

For a moment, he almost imagined a spark, enough that he said the dumbest thing. "Stay. Close the door and come over here to untie me." No sooner spoken than a sigh escaped him. *What am I doing?* To his disgust, he couldn't bring himself to tell her to leave. Oh no, like a dog who enjoyed a whipping, he ordered her to come closer.

Because apparently, I've learned to enjoy torture. The erotic kind at least.

What happened to remaining far away from the doctor? Sure, the decision to escape her presence had been born the night before during a hazy liquor-lust-and-anger-induced moment, but inebriated or not, he stood by that decision. With her near, he would most certainly lose his mind—and control of his wolf.

The door slammed shut, and she took a step toward him.

"Leave," he barked.

Confusion crossed her face as she halted. "I thought you just said to untie you."

"I shouldn't have asked. It's not your job. You should leave."

For a moment, she stood there as a myriad of emotions ran lightning quick over her face. Resolve firmed her shoulders, and she closed the distance to his bed. "Listen, I know things kind of got out of hand last night."

"Do you think?" was his sarcastic drawl. "As I recall, my hands almost got you out of your pants, which we both know would have been a bad thing."

"Yes, that would have been a bad idea."

It shouldn't have hurt when she agreed, yet a pang still struck him. He couldn't help a bitter laugh. "No woman wants a man who can't finish the job."

"That's not what I meant, and you know it. Only an idiot would think I wasn't enjoying myself." Look at those cheeks turn red.

"Calling me an idiot now? Nice bedside manner."

His retort dragged her expression even lower.

She truly was perturbed. "And there you hit the reason on the head. I am supposed to be treating you, not making out with you."

"Some would have called it healing. Sexual healing."

"Sexual healing isn't supposed to be hands-on."

"Mostly lips," he interjected. "But continue." Continue to regret the moment they shared the previous night. The moment that he relived over and over and fucking over in his dreams and awake. For once, when he closed his eyes, he didn't see just death and despair. But opening them meant facing the reality that he couldn't have the woman he wanted.

"What I did with you, in the van after the outing, was wrong. As in lose my professional license wrong."

As she rejected him, no matter how nicely, he couldn't help but lash out. "Wrong and reputation crushing. I can just imagine the mockery you'd suffer from your peers if they knew you let a cripple diddle you."

"Don't be gross," she snapped, her hands hesitating over the first strap tethering him. She fixed him with a laser-green glare. "You will stop talking about yourself like that because that's not how I see you."

Don't say it. Don't ask. "And how do you see me?" *You fool. Why would you do that?*

Lips flattened as she copped out instead of answering. "I see you as my patient because I am your doctor."

"You and I both know you very nicely

skirted that question. Answer it."

"I did. I think we both need to remind ourselves that I'm your doctor, and that means there are certain things I can't say. Or do."

Yet she felt the same urges, he'd wager. He'd smelled the honey sweetness of her desire the previous night and on other occasions. The idea she desired him and fought it should elate, but instead, it deflated. He should take the out she gave him. Use the wall she wanted to erect based on their doctor-patient relationship and hide behind it. He should have helped her maintain a distance between them.

But...*I want to know how she sees me.* It seemed of the utmost importance. "If you insist on playing the inappropriate card, then fine, I fire you. We are no longer doctor/patient. Answer the damned question. How do you see me?"

"You are not going to bully me into telling you." She slipped the cuff free from his wrist, and he clenched his fist by his side, lest it do something it shouldn't such as tug the red lock of hair dangling.

"Would a guilt trip work instead?"

"Nope." She moved around to the other side of the wide bed to reach his other hand. Wise choice. He might not have been able to stop himself from lunging for a kiss if she leaned over him.

No kissing.

On one thing she was absolutely right, just not for the reason she thought. *I don't give a rat's ass if she's my doctor.* Knowing who she was, what she was, his mate, meant there was almost no barrier he wouldn't cross, no rule he wouldn't break to claim her.

Therein lay the problem. He couldn't claim

her, but for a moment the previous night, he'd forgotten. Alcohol had lowered his defenses, and he got a taste of what could have been, if he weren't half a man. *Red will never be my mate.*

Why? His wolf truly didn't understand. Why couldn't they have Janine? It felt so right when he held her in his arms.

But right didn't change fact. This wasn't a fantasy world, where unicorns shit rainbows and Derrick could walk on two legs and write his name in the snow with pee. This was reality, and in this reality, his two hands were free, Janine—with her delectable scent and temptation—remained in reach and he couldn't handle it.

She had to leave, and yet she seemed determined to stay. Time to make her go. Only if she left could he perhaps regain some equilibrium. How to chase her from his room, though? Mere words never seemed to bug her.

Only one thing ever completely flustered her.

Before he could tell himself what a bad idea it was, he grabbed Janine. Lunged really. His hands grasped her around the hips and drew her abruptly to him, tumbling her onto the bed on top of his body.

He let himself enjoy it for the seconds it would last.

A gasp escaped her parted lips, yet his red-haired downfall did nothing to push herself away. She remained lying almost full length on his frame. Her breasts squishing against his chest, the scent of her—which he inhaled, eyes closed—so damned perfect. He couldn't help but sniff again.

"Now you are being totally creepy," she said.

"I know shifters rely a lot on scent, but snorting it like it's some kind of mind-blowing drug is not the most sane thing you could do."

The sassy retort startled a rusty chuckle from him. "This is actually a very normal thing to do among those who know what we are. It is hiding my true self among the humans that is the falseness of who I am."

Her turn to snicker. "That was very Zen."

"I had an uncle who used to say that to me. Said his shrink loved it when he said that shit."

"Lying to me only hurts you."

"Now who's quoting bullshit?" He opened his eyes and found himself caught in hers.

"I'm the shrink, remember? I'm supposed to say corny stuff."

Problem was her corny expressions just served to draw him further under her spell. The more he discovered about Janine, the more torturous it proved. Such cruelty to have her lush frame flush against him and yet unable to do a damned thing about it. The reminder moved his hands from her waist to her ass.

Tug. He yanked her hard against him. "If I said I want you, what would you say?"

Reject me. Reject me. Help him regain some pride and aide him in walking away.

Instead, he could have howled in disbelief as the faint pheromones of her arousal tickled his senses.

He could smell it. She wanted him. And yet what did she say?

"I'd say that desire for a woman is a good sign for you. That your mindset is adapting to the fact that not everything is out of reach."

"I don't just desire any woman. I. Want. You." He growled the words, agitation building in him as she tried to stay aloof. It bothered him that she lied about her attraction to him. She did see him as less than a man.

I don't want to let her go. His fingers squeezed the flesh of her rounded ass, and he rumbled low as he ground her against him, the top part of him so aroused and wanting, yet the lower half so dead.

He uttered a pained cry and released her, pushing her away from him. She should have run away.

I want her to go away.

Instead of fleeing, Janine grabbed his cheeks and forced his gaze. Eyes the clear green of a spring meadow gentled his beast. "Stop it."

He growled.

Fine dark brows drew close as she frowned. "Don't you growl at me, mister. You are the one misbehaving."

"I fired you. Go away." The petulance in his voice surely only happened because he didn't have access to his balls.

"You can't fire me. I don't work for you."

"Yeah, you work for the council, which your stepfather happens to work on. You kind of omitted that."

"I did, and for good reason. It has nothing to do with our professional relationship."

"I think it does, and at any rate, I asked your father to remove you."

"I know. He told me to come home."

For a moment, knowing someone threatened

to send her away brought a hot rage on him. *Yet isn't that what I wanted? She needs to leave.*

I don't want her to go.

Fuck.

Having her near messed with what little brain function he had left. The only time he'd ever felt dumber was when his blood used to go south. Janine gave him brain erections. Snort.

"Are you laughing?"

He abruptly stopped, which probably didn't appear any saner than his previous giggling. "You said your dad tried to have you leave, yet you're still here. Is this goodbye?"

Don't whimper. Don't you dare fucking whimper like a newborn pup.

"No, it's not goodbye. I'm not going anywhere until we convince my dad you're not a menace to society."

Rewind. What? "He said that?"

"Not in so many words, but I know Orson. He's ruthless if he thinks our kind is threatened."

"As he should be." Derrick wouldn't even argue the importance of keeping their secret. "And your stepfather is right. I am a menace to society." A menace to her.

Because if I can't have her, someone else might. And that can't happen either. He might not believe in suicide, but he could probably murder.

"You're not dangerous."

"Yes, I am. Come a little closer, and I'll show you." He snapped his teeth.

She crossed her arms. "Are you doing this on purpose to agitate me so I leave?"

"Yes. No. Maybe. Are you as confused as I

am?" he asked, fascinated by the soft part of her lips.

"Not really because I can tell you're doing it on purpose to drive me away."

"Can you blame me? Kind of still naked over here. What's a man got to do in order to achieve some privacy and dignity?"

The red blush on her cheeks as he drew her gaze to his groin warmed him from the waist up. Below the waist, his flaccid body looked so unassuming.

"I'm sorry. I should let you get dressed." She walked away from the bed and took a moment staring outside the window.

Clothing was overrated, especially on her. One thing for sure, if the roles were reversed and she were naked, he wouldn't be gentlemanly enough to give her some privacy to get dressed. Hell, he'd probably toss the damned garments away just to keep her naked.

But she wasn't the one naked. He was. And his dick at repose was not something he should flop around in.

He sat up and stretched as he cast about for something to wear. He recalled wheeling himself in here the previous night and, after a visit to the bathroom—where he cursed the tubes he needed to use—flinging the garments around. He'd splayed himself on the bed and managed one cuff before the orderly arrived and attached the other. Given his agitation and the alcohol still working through his system, he didn't dare sleep unfettered.

A glimpse of fabric caught his attention. He leaned over and grabbed it with the tips of his fingers. Aha. A shirt.

Upper body covered, he peered around for a below-the-belt covering. Janine stood at the window, a shapely delight in her form-fitting black slacks and the pink blouse tucked into them, leaving her ass in full view.

He noted the leg of his track pants and pushed himself over on the bed to grab them. "You know, it occurs to me that you never did say why you came barging in so early. Or were you lying? Were you trying to get a peek at the goods? Not much to see, I'll admit. Not anymore. In its day, though, my sword was impressive."

She ignored his crassness. "Are you decent?"

"Not really. I'd call myself borderline passable." His attempt at humor fell flat.

She whirled. "The reason I'm here is because I needed to tell you we're going on another road trip later today."

"So soon? Are you trying to turn me into a lush? Was this whole argument about you being my doctor and me your patient a lie? Or do you only take advantage of me when you've had a few? No need to get drunk to fuck me unless you need it to forget my lack of legs. Or was it my oral skills you were interested in?" He waggled his tongue. Crude, but desperation made him resort to it in an effort to have her leave. How could he think and resist with her still too damned close.

A moue of pursed lips didn't show her impressed by his offer. "That is not attractive or enticing at all. And to answer some of your inane questions, you won't be getting drunk. I'll be making sure of that. But this will probably be an overnighter given the distance."

He froze. "I can't leave overnight yet." Not with the way the nightmares hit.

"You can and will be, with me, today. I got permission."

"But I won't want to." Yeah that sounded petulantly childish.

"You have to." She planted her hands on her hips. "Enough of the stubborn crap and woe-is-me comments about yourself. The situation is serious. After your phone call to him last night, my dad thinks you're unstable."

"Because I tried to do the right thing and send you away?" Who knew doing such an annoyingly honorable thing would show off his insanity the best?

"Is sending me away the right thing? You said last night I was your mate."

She just had to bring up the giant elephant between them. He'd hoped she'd not heard or at least misunderstood. Nope. She'd caught his words. "Drunken rambling." He lied. *I am so totally her mate.* That never became more clear than at the moment of the kiss.

Derrick had thought, make that hoped, he could escape the curse of the mating fever, but he got barbed with a hook and could feel himself getting reeled in.

A part of him had hoped the feeling had been exacerbated by the booze. Then she walked in and killed that hope. *I want her more now than ever.*

"Are you lying to me?" she asked.

Yes, just like he was lying to himself about Janine. He could try and send her away all he wanted. As he'd learned overnight, Janine didn't have to be present for him to hunger.

He might not suffer from an erection and blue balls, but his every waking thought was of Janine. Being around her left him in an odd state of arousal. A head-to-waist awareness that amplified everything around him and made him yearn for more…

He didn't understand this kind of lust. Doubted her claim that he could satisfy it. Was he doomed to die of horniness?

And he couldn't even talk about it to her because he'd already said too much.

"I thought we ascertained that shit happened last night that shouldn't have. Why don't we leave it at that?" His turn to try and pretend it hadn't occurred.

"We can't completely ignore the fact that last night things got pretty intense."

"And now, today, we're doing that awkward dance."

A wan smile tugged at her lips. "Yes, this is a tad uncomfortable, but we're both adults. We can handle it. Especially since I bear most of the responsibility. I should have acted more professionally. So, please forgive me for not behaving with more decorum. It won't ever happen again, I promise you. I hope we can move past that aberration and focus on more important things."

More important than her calling their interlude an aberration? That stung. "Talk about putting the cripple in his place. You kissed me out of pity so I wouldn't guess, but the truth is finally coming out. You don't find me attractive." His accusation didn't match what he remembered smelling, but he still flung it at her.

"Is that what you think?"

He didn't know what to think. When they talked, he could go on for hours. Hell, he could sit there staring at her forever. The scent of her drugged him, and every time she found an excuse to push him away, it was like a dagger stabbing him over and over.

She sighed when he didn't reply. "I guess I have sent mixed signals, and you do deserve the truth." She peeked down at her hands, the fingers nervously weaving and unweaving. "I like you, Derrick. A lot more than a doctor should care for her patient. I feel things for you, things I shouldn't feel. That's why I kissed you."

"So you kissed me because…" He couldn't say it.

"Because I like you."

"And you enjoyed the kiss?" Because he just had to dig the dagger deeper. *Yeah, because knowing how much she liked it will so make letting her go easier.*

A smile pulled her lips softly. "Oh, I enjoyed it. More than I should admit. But it was wrong of me to have done it. You're in a vulnerable stage right now. I know better than to take advantage."

"I was there too, you know, and I can promise you, Doc, you weren't doing anything I didn't already want." Still wanted. Didn't matter how often he told himself that he didn't want her to stay. A part of him wanted to wrap himself around her and never let her go.

"Of course you want sexual touching. As I keep explaining to you, you're a healthy young man still in his prime. By accident, I've awakened you to the fact you're still desirable with lots to give a woman. It just can't be me."

"Don't I get a say?" Why did he keep going from determination to keep her at arm's length to trying to change her mind?

"Maybe if circumstances were different and I wasn't your doctor and we'd just met, we could make a go of it, but right now, as it stands, we have to keep things on a professional level."

Too late for that. "And what if not having you is the thing that sets my wolf off?" Blackmail? Better than letting her think she could just push him away.

She didn't fall for it. "I think you can control your wolf just fine."

"Don't bet on it."

"I am betting on it because tonight you need to prove to my dad and anyone else watching that you're more man than wolf, and I'm not joking when I say your life depends on it."

"What exactly are you dragging me to? A hearing? Some kind of tribunal in front of the council?" A firing squad?

"Worse. I'm taking you to a twentieth wedding anniversary for my parents."

No amount of arguing changed her mind. She left his room, her parting words, "I'll pick you up around one. Be ready."

But I don't want to go. Screw the party. Screw her dad. Screw her.

Fuck, I wish I could screw her.

He paced his room, which involved rolling a few feet, pivoting, and rolling back. It didn't ease his agitation. The clock kept ticking, a countdown to her return.

He visited the pool. The gym. Took himself for a rapid wheel around the grounds. The agitation followed, and more minutes fled past, along with an hour, two, three…

The list of many reasons why he shouldn't go, of why he should stay away from Janine grew in his mind. *She deserves a whole man. I'm not stable. I don't have a job, just a disability check. I need restraints at night.*

Yet all his arguments kept getting squashed by one conviction—*she's mine.*

Which was why at one p.m., he sat outside beside the van they'd used the night before.

At one-fifteen, she came stalking toward him. When she got within a few yards, she grumbled, "I've been looking everywhere for you."

"You said we were leaving at one. I assumed you meant by vehicle. Hence why I waited for you right here."

"I didn't expect you to actually go without a fight."

"Are you blaming me for being late?" he said in mock shock. The evil eye she gave him drew a chuckle. "Lucky for you, Red, I'm kind of in the mood for a road trip."

The quirky reply narrowed her gaze. "Why do you seem so eager to go? You should be arguing against it."

"Just being a good patient for my doctor." A wide grin split his lips as he wheeled himself up the ramp into the van. Janine might have concocted a plan, but Derrick had one too.

Get her removed as his doctor and his life before he did something monumentally stupid.

Like fall in love.
Too late.

Chapter Twelve

Despite the mishap in locating Derrick—*I really thought I'd have to hunt him down and force him*—the road trip passed rather peacefully. Despite the sexual tension between them, there was also a genuine like for one another, and when he wasn't barbing her or trying to push Janine away, they could have the most interesting conversations.

It passed the long trip. While Derrick started out driving, the highway part of the route being the longest, she took over once they hit an exit. She made sure to give him a pit stop so he could use a washroom, and she said not a word about the fact that he took a few minutes longer than other people to do his business and glared at those who dared to complain outside the locked door.

As she took the familiar twists and turns to her parents' house, she couldn't help a touch of anxiousness. How would her stepdad react? With her, Orson was the most lovable teddy bear a girl could ask for, but with anyone he thought threatened her? Poor Jeremy wouldn't even look at her in the hallways of school after that time he dared call her an ugly name.

But Derrick isn't a threat to me. Unless losing her heart counted.

Pulling up in front of her parents' place, she slowed the car.

Derrick let out a low whistle. "That is some house," he said.

A shrug rolled through her shoulders. "I guess. All the houses in this area are kind of big. Suburbia at its finest." Set on an acre, with protected parkland at the back of the property, the house was a two-story colonial style with giant white columns in the front and a façade of windows. It might look impressive to some, but to her, it was home.

"The place looks massive," he mumbled as she eased the car in behind a dark blue BMW.

"It is a decent size, and really nice inside," she admitted. "As a councilmember, Orson entertains a lot. Apparently, it's important when we have visitors, especially from other countries, or even the occasional wild group that doesn't necessarily recognize council rule, that we impress them."

"So you had a lot of strangers and shifters coming in and out of your life as a kid? That must have been interesting, or did you even know what they were? You never did tell me how you found out your stepdad was a bear. Did he just come out and tell you? I thought the admission of our existence was strictly prohibited."

"It's not allowed, but he and my mom had to do something the night I caught her outside hugging a bear in the yard. I'd gone to get a drink of water from the bathroom and saw them from a window. I ran outside screaming and begging for the bear not to eat my mom. At that point, I still had nightmares about my dad dying. Orson felt horrible about my panic and changed right then and there. Which, of course, made me scream more. Once they calmed me down, he and my mom explained what he was. It took me a few days of thinking it over and hiding from him before he sought me out as his bear."

"He did what! Is the man delusional? How could he think that was a good idea?" The words emerged with angry vehemence.

Hastening to reassure him, she didn't think and put her hand out, touching his arm. An electric thrill shocked her. Did he feel it too? He certainly went still, and to cover the moment and her gaffe, she continued her story. "You make it sound awful when it wasn't. It was actually very sweet."

"Coming face-to-face with a bear is sweet?" The sarcasm dripped.

"It is when it has a great big bow around his neck, which matched the bow on the teddy that he brought with his teeth. Little girls are suckers for cute things." Even grumpy ones. She drew away her hand and cleared her throat. "So there was this giant bear, with a little teddy in his mouth, and he lay down in front of me. Didn't eat me. Or growl. Or roar. And I didn't pee my pants, so things were going pretty good. Anyhow, Orson lay there who knows how long until I had the courage to grab that teddy. Once I did that and he didn't eat me, I figured what the heck and petted him." But she still remembered the frightened thrill of reaching out her hand and letting her fingers sift the short coarse hair on his back. The soft touch of the fur tucked behind his ears. The man practically purred like a cat if you rubbed them right.

"You petted a councilmember like he was a dog?" Derrick snickered, trying to not allow himself to be moved by that special moment.

She didn't allow him to mock the kind act because she knew Derrick was capable of the same kindness. "Don't disparage what happened. Orson is a good man. A good father. He showed a little girl that, despite the fact he could turn into a ferocious beast, it didn't mean he would ever hurt me. Just like he'd never hurt my mother. Inside the bear, it is still him."

"Is this the part where I cry and admit that inside this broken body I'm still me?" He might speak the words with arrogant disdain, but she saw how his fingers clenched tight, the knuckles turning white. "Is this where I tell you I'm nothing like your father?"

"You are nothing like my father."

"I disagree. I think your father and I have a lot in common. Let's say we look past the fact we both lost mobility and our minds from our ordeals. Those aren't the only commonalities. We both pushed family away."

"Did you? I mean, you never saw your family until I brought your niece and nephew. You wouldn't let them see you at all once you returned. And they haven't pushed the issue"—a frown creased her forehead—"which, given I've met your sister, and spoken to your mother, surprises me." It seemed out of character for them not to barge in and force Derrick to see them. She'd only dared to ask Mrs. Grayson once why she didn't just show up. After all, so many people lived by the adage it was easier to beg forgiveness than ask permission.

Mrs. Grayson had replied, "Right now he's hurt and licking his wounds. Pushing him too hard might tip him over an edge he can't return from. I had that happen to a brother of mine. We learned that sometimes the best thing we can do to help is give some space."

A respectful move on the part of his family, people with whom he shared an intense emotional connection. One wrong move from them could destroy him, and yet, a doctor could push those boundaries. A doctor could challenge him because he could lash out and he wouldn't feel the guilt that he would with family.

"My family knows how to leave me alone."

She giggled. "Having met them, I can't believe you said that."

A smile tugged at his lips. "They are a tad much at times to handle." The smile turned upside down. "Which is why I've kept them away."

"I guess you and my dad do have something in common. You're both so caught up in your own misery you can't see how it hurts those who care for you. And that was the point about my story with Orson. Sure, he was scared to expose his innermost self to me. To let me see him as he was. But he didn't let that stop him, and showed me how much he trusted me with his love. He loved me more than my dad ever did." The vulnerable admission spilled from her before she could stop it.

"Your dad loved you. I know he did." The affront in his tone shone clearly. "He just wasn't thinking right when he came back."

"I know that now." She cast him a glance sideways. "But at the time, I didn't. What else is a little girl supposed to think when her father comes back from the war and doesn't talk to her? I was only seven years old. I didn't understand why. Why he didn't tuck me in at night anymore. Why he didn't swing me in the air and then hug me tight saying everything would be okay? What is a little girl to think but she's the fault when her dad cries at the sight of her? Every time I tried to give him a hug, he pushed me away." Her words caught in a sob, and she inhaled sharply, a hiccup of sound, feeling the scalding moisture clinging to her lashes. "And then…"

"Don't." He held out his hand to her in a plea.

Ignoring it proved easy once she dropped her gaze to her hands. He couldn't stop her now. Let him hear the ugly truth. Perhaps he needed to hear it.

She took a deep, shuddering breath. "And then my dad leaves. He leaves again, for good this time. Leaves me. Leaves my mom and everything changed. Everything. Again. I was so sad. So lost, and I thought." Oh how she'd thought too much back then. "No, I didn't think. I was convinced it was something that I did that sent my dad away. Or maybe it was something I didn't do." She spread her hands wide, forcing a smile on her lips for a mirth she didn't feel. "Who knows why he did it? The fact is my daddy left me."

"War changes a man."

"It does." She peeked at him from under damp lashes. "No one is denying that your experiences change you, and they hurt you. They even redefine who you are, but you can't let that control your life."

"And here's the speech." He rolled his eyes.

"Yes, the speech. Because, while you're

wallowing in self-pity, I lived on the other side of that coin. I was that family member who was pushed away by someone she loved. The same way you keep pushing folks away."

"How is letting them in supposed to help me or them? I mean, let's look at your situation for a second. When your dad was around, everyone was miserable. Your dad leaves, and that left the door open for your stepfather to swoop in and give you a happily-ever-after."

He poked at the injury she still bore from her father's suicide. "Yes, my life turned out great, but not without a lot of pain. And here's the thing. If my daddy had gotten the help he needed and learned to cope, we could have been happy."

Again, he honed in with precision. "Is it that could-have-been that makes you choose to work with men just like your father? Assuaging a lingering guilt?"

She looked away from him, fingers clenched around the steering wheel, even though the engine was long shut off. "I will never completely lose that guilt, and yes, you could say I am still trying to atone for what happened to my father. Because I never want another little girl to suffer like I suffered. I won't fail again."

"So fixing me, fixing other trauma survivors, we're just a means to an end for you. A feel-good pill."

"Of course not," she hastened to say, but Derrick didn't listen. He squeezed between the seats of the minivan and made his way to the back.

"Don't watch me," he barked.

How did he know she watched? He never

looked back once. She faced forward, staring through the windshield and noting she'd missed the lilacs blooming. A mundane thought to try and regain her equilibrium after that grand confession. "I'm not doing this out of pity," she said as she listened to him get in his chair and open the tailgate.

"You're doing this because it's a job."

"I never denied that." She clambered out of the minivan and made her way to the back just in time to see him dumping himself into his already flipped open chair. *How does he do it that quickly?* "From day one, I never said I was anything other than a psychologist."

"A psychologist with daddy issues."

"So what? It doesn't mean I can't do my job. On the contrary, my experience makes me more determined than ever to help you."

"You can help me by going away. I don't need your save-the-cripple mentality."

There came the cruel words, as, once again, he sought to push her away. As if she'd let that happen. She leaned forward and braced her hands on either side of his chair, effectively locking him into place unless he physically knocked her away. She'd wager too much of a gentleman resided inside Derrick for him to lay violent hands on her.

She caught his gaze. "Listen, I might have gone into medicine because of my childhood and my dad, but just because I let that experience guide some of my actions, it doesn't make my emotions any less. I'm not just doing this because it's work. I care about you."

"You care about me like you would care about anybody who's broken," he replied. "I'm not special to you. I'm nothing to you but another guy with mental issues, and it was stupid of me to think otherwise."

She wanted to reassure him and tell him how different everything was with him. Emotionally invested for sure, and yet, she couldn't admit it out loud and give weight to the feelings. Once the truth emerged, then she would have no choice. She'd have to leave as his doctor. But she couldn't say nothing, not with him obviously hurting. "You are special."

"Stop it. I don't want to hear it. I know what I am now."

"What are you?" she asked.

He let his gaze meet hers. "I am just a patient."

And with a rapid twist, he reversed away from her before spinning and heading to the house.

A good thing he left rapidly because she couldn't stop a whisper. "You're more than that to me."

He meant way too much to her, and to hear him say, with a sadness he probably never intended for her to notice, that he meant nothing, twisted her heart. She'd hurt him, even though it was the last thing she wanted to do.

The heaviness in her heart lingered as she followed Derrick to the front door of the home she used to run through when younger. Each step did nothing to ease the turmoil in her.

She wanted to yell at him that she wished things were different. That over the course of the past few weeks she'd grown to care for him more than she should. She'd made the classic mistake of falling in love.

Dear God, I love him. Loved a patient. So much for the right thing and ethics.

No wonder he complained about confusion. She was just as confused. She didn't know how to stop these burgeoning emotions she had for him. She didn't know how to deal with him, not as a patient, but a man. *What should I do? He said I was his mate. What if it's true? What if I'm doing more damage pushing him away?*

What if he was wrong, though? What if he just thought of her as his mate because she was the first woman he'd showed an interest in since his ordeal? Either way, the right thing to do involved walking away from Derrick and letting another doctor take over, one that was not emotionally involved.

A doctor that wouldn't give a damn if Derrick lived or died.

I can't do it. Utterly selfish of her, but she couldn't walk away. *I can't, because if something happened and I wasn't there, I will blame myself.*

What an epiphany to have, and moments before she'd have to face the scrutiny of her parents. The double doors, thick and darkly stained wood, loomed before them. More ominous, the moment of truth with her stepdad awaited. At least there wasn't a crowd, yet, for the party. Janine had ensured they would arrive a bit earlier. The extra time would give Orson and Derrick a chance to talk.

At least she hoped they would talk. With Derrick, who knew what might happen? Sure, he'd done well at the bar the night before, but another outing, so soon and with such dangerous implications? It could end up in disaster, especially considering the glower on Derrick's face.

I think I screwed up. I don't think I should have brought him. But the realization came too late. The door opened, and there stood her mother and stepfather, bright smiles of welcome on their faces.

"June-bug, you made it." Orson held open his arms, and she couldn't resist the comfort they always offered. She dove forward and buried herself against his big chest for a teddy bear hug that never failed to make her feel better. Then it was her mother's turn to squeeze her tight and whisper, "So glad you could come."

As if Janine would miss this event. She'd spoken the truth to Derrick earlier when she related how she'd thought her mother would never find happiness again. Orson changed all that—and for the better. Her mother glowed with contentment.

Much as it pained Janine to admit, Derrick was right about her having a better life with Orson. Even if her father had healed, she remembered enough of his behavior before he'd left to know Orson was a much better father and husband than her biological father ever had been. The very thought never failed to douse her in guilt. It seemed wrong that she loved Orson more.

Her stepdad fixed his gaze on the man in the wheelchair, and yes, he had to look slightly down, but their less-than-equal height didn't stop the war of dominance between Orson and Derrick. When it came to strong wills, they were equals, the pair of them staring, bristling predators looking to determine who would prevail.

How interesting that Derrick chose to pit himself against someone of Orson's stature in the shifter world. The teachings she'd received at her stepdad's knee indicated a certain hierarchy. The strong, and intelligent, not just brutes, ruled the others. Some shifters lived in packs with alphas or, in the case of the lions out in Vegas, a king. Others lived in scattered communities that answered only to the higher council rules. As for who sat on the council? Only the strongest.

Orson was strong, and not just because he shifted into an over-eight-foot-tall bear and could crush a man in his grip. He ruled in will.

Yet Derrick won when it came to stubbornness, and the doctor inside her was pleased to see he didn't back down, even if there was a height disadvantage. And, yes, she knew how that bothered him, an understandable feeling, given he'd spent a good portion of his life looking down on others, not badly, but because he stood so tall.

Now Derrick had to sit, and yet the wheelchair did not make him look weak. With his expression fierce, he exuded strength. He also appeared vital, and healthy, the pallor she'd noted in his skin upon her first arrival replaced with a healthier color, perhaps because of their many walks. He also spent more time on his grooming, the wild, unkempt man she'd first met replaced with a clean-shaven jaw and brush-cut hair. For the occasion, he'd also put on a collared polo knit shirt and khakis. For all his grumbling, Derrick was starting to show vanity about his appearance.

"You must be Derrick Grayson. I'm Orson Whelan. Welcome to my home."

Derrick arched brow. "Welcome? More like dragged."

"I did not drag you," she muttered. "Just insisted, vehemently."

Orson coughed behind his hand. "Yes, June-bug can be quite tenacious when she's convinced of something."

"A pity she's wrong in this instance. Your daughter is too softhearted."

"On that we are agreed."

Look at that, Derrick and her dad bonding over the fact they thought she was a mushy idiot. At least they were talking. A good start.

"Why don't we move indoors to chat," said her mother. "The skitters are starting to come out, and besides, the couches are much more comfortable than standing."

"Nadine is right. You should come in." Orson and her mother stepped out of the way. Derrick grandly gestured for Janine to go in first. "After you, Doctor."

"You better not be planning to run away," she stated, moving ahead.

"And miss this fun-filled evening? Why, Red, don't you trust me? Oh, that's right, you don't because you're the lunatic's *doctor.* " The word spoken in a sneer.

"I am tempted to have them withhold your pudding," she snapped back over her shoulder, only to realize in the silence right after that her words were heard by more than just Derrick.

Janine couldn't have said who muffled a snort—Orson, her mother—didn't matter. Talk about behaving most unprofessionally. Simply par for the course where Derrick was concerned.

Stepping through the arch immediately to the

left, she found herself in the formal living room, which adjoined the dining room. Growing up, she well recalled how these were the off-limits rooms. No playing allowed in here. The forbidden nature of it meant even tiptoeing to run a hand over the gleaming wood furniture gave her a secret thrill. The chandelier with its dozens of lights glittered on the rare occasion when she ate in the dining room with the adults. Totally awe-inspiring until she got old enough to realize sitting with the grownups wasn't as much fun as being plopped on a kitchen stool with cable television and access to the best tidbits of the meal.

A quick glance around the room and she noted Derrick shouldn't have much problem maneuvering. The furniture sat well spaced with lots of room to get around.

For some reason, her pulse fluttered, a nervous ticking she couldn't quite understand. Sure, this meeting with Orson was important, and yet, if this were any other man she'd brought, she'd almost call it trepidation. The kind of trepidation a girl felt when bringing home a boy she liked for the first time.

I like him. I just can't be with him. She perched on a couch and pressed her hands on her knees, the fabric of her skirt covering them. Her parents chose to sit side-by-side across from her while Derrick took a position between the two, just outside of the circle formed by the furniture.

"How was the drive up?"

"Did you see much construction?"

Small talk, the bane of polite society, no wonder Derrick rolled his eyes. Her parents filled in the gap of silence with trivial chatter.

Derrick, with his blunt nature, was having none of that. "Now that we're all gathered, why don't we just cut to the chase and discuss why I'm really here? Should I live or die? I know what my answer is, but I do hope I'll be allowed to eat first."

"Don't be such a drama king," Janine exclaimed. "No one is dying, so stop it."

"But you can't deny I'm broken." Derrick spread his hands in a helpless gesture. "If the king's men couldn't put Humpty Dumpty together again, then what do you think a human doctor can do?" He daggered the words in her direction, intentionally trying to hurt her.

The angle on her chin went from posture perfect to stubborn because she recalled using this analogy on him when they first met. How dare he throw it back at her? "You are not an egg."

"Nope. I'm a Lycan, one with a very thin control. I know that. You know that. And I'm pretty sure our dear councilman over here knows that. I'll bet he's been getting some pretty juicy reports about my behavior. We all know what has to happen to the unstable."

"You're not unstable."

"Says you. I disagree."

She blinked at him before retorting. "You can't disagree because I'm the doctor."

"And doctor knows best," he said in clear mockery. "Except, in this case, you don't. I am bad news, Red."

"I think you're intentionally being aggravating."

He leaned forward in his chair. "Aggravating?

Is that the best you can do?"

"Would you prefer asshat? Because you're definitely displaying anal characteristics!"

"Isn't name calling your patients against your code of ethics?" he snapped back.

"Don't you throw my ethics at me because you're frustrated…" The word emerged slowly as she suddenly remembered the audience. Any possibility her parents hadn't noticed their argument?

"I really should start getting the food out. Would someone like a drink or a snack?" her mother said in the sudden stillness.

"Food sounds like a fine idea," Derrick announced. "A man going to the gallows is entitled to a final meal, and a drink right about now would be welcome. A double, if it's not too much trouble."

Her stepdad's lips tightened into a flat line. "A final decision has not yet been rendered regarding your situation."

"Just delaying the inevitable," Derrick said with shake of his head.

Before Janine could think twice, she leaned over and punched his arm.

His eyes rounded in surprise. "Ow. You hit me. What kind of therapy is that?"

"It's called the stop-talking-like-you're-dying one."

"We're all dying, Red. Some just sooner than others."

"Do you want to die?" It wasn't Janine who asked, but rather Orson.

Attention drawn, Derrick faced her stepdad. "No. I don't actually."

"Yet you seem to think your actions will get you killed?"

Derrick shrugged. "For all my daytime progress, at night, the nightmares are bad. I'm sure you've read the reports."

A dip of the head as Orson confirmed it. "I have read some, and the ones I've seen are not favorable. You are restrained most nights, and there are issues with your wolf pushing to the surface. It seems your control is tenuous at best."

"He's not dangerous," she blurted. "I've seen him at night. I woke him from a nightmare, and he didn't hurt me. He is not a danger."

"That's not for you to decide." Derrick growled it before Orson could.

"Do we have to talk about this now?" asked her mother.

The vehement yeses came from more than one mouth.

"Might as well get this chat over with before our guests arrive. It is, after all, why June-bug brought her guest. It won't take long." Her stepdad turned his gaze on Derrick. "According to reports, your wolf is simmering close to the surface. True or false?"

"True." Derrick didn't explain any further. Didn't explain he'd kept his wolf penned for fear of shifting a fragment in his back. He didn't tell her stepdad that his wolf was probably feeling caged and frustrated. On second thought, probably better if he didn't.

"The reports also say that you require nightly tethering. Have you been shifting into your wolf during your sleep?"

"No. But in the throes of my nightmares, I sometimes don't always recognize friend from foe. The tethers keep me from making a mistake."

"Have you attacked anyone since your return?"

She jumped in. "Enough with the interrogation. I'm telling you, not as your daughter but as a doctor that he's not dangerous, Dad. I wouldn't have brought him to our home if I thought he was."

"You would if you were too emotionally invested," her stepdad replied. "Reports on his behavior are not the only ones I've been reading. I know about your current unorthodox treatment of him. You have not been meeting him in an office. On the contrary, you have been gallivanting around the grounds with him and even off grounds. If I didn't know better, I would almost say you were dating him."

Derrick protested before she could. "Date? Never. I would never saddle Janine, or anyone else for that matter, with a cripple."

She punched him again. "Stop calling yourself that. I've already told you I don't care about the fact you're in the wheelchair. I'm not that shallow. You know why we can't be together."

A silence fell after that as the admission echoed around the room. She noted the sly smirk on Derrick's face. That jerk. She hit him again, the physical venting something she usually never condoned, but Derrick needed the jolt.

"Hey, this is abuse," he exclaimed.

"Damned straight it is for doing that on purpose. You made me admit I took advantage of you. You're trying to get me taken off your case."

"Doing better than trying, Red. Succeeded."

"I'll be the judge of that," Orson interjected. He fixed a contemplative gaze on Derrick. "Honey," he said, addressing Janine's mother, "weren't you going to start putting out the food? Our guests will be arriving soon. Take June-bug with you to give you a hand."

Janine folded her arms. "Could you be more obvious about trying to get rid of me?"

"Obvious would be me saying get out so I can talk your boyfriend here."

"I am not her boyfriend."

Immediate denial by Derrick and, while the correct answer, a part of her didn't like hearing it said aloud, not one bit.

"What are you going to ask him that I can't hear? I am, after all, his doctor."

"Not for this conversation you aren't. So get your ass in the kitchen." When she wouldn't budge, Orson softened his expression. "I won't hurt him, June-bug. Promise."

The trust she had in her stepdad's word was the only thing that budged her. Despite her trepidation, she let her mother grab her by the hand and drag her into the kitchen. *I don't know if I should leave those two alone.* However, the purpose of this trip was for her dad to realize Derrick didn't pose a menace to society.

The problem was, would Derrick cooperate? She couldn't be sure what Derrick would say or do with her stepdad. He seemed hell-bent on getting Janine out of his life, more than was normal for a patient who struggled with treatment.

Except let's be honest here. He doesn't want to get rid of me because he doesn't like me as a doctor. He wants to get rid of me because he wants to be with me but thinks he can't.

She couldn't help recalling what he'd said. *He called me his mate.* Drunken rambling or did it hold some truth? And if it did, what did it mean? Was it possible he was mistaken?

What did it say about her confused emotions that a part of her fluttered at the thought of being his mate?

She peeked at her mother, crouched and buried in the fridge, pulling out covered platters and a pre-made pitcher of punch.

"Mom, can I ask you something?"

"You know you can ask me anything."

"When you met Orson, did it feel…" Janine paused as she tried to figure out a way to say it.

"Feel what?"

"Different. As if there was something different about him. Something that let you know he was the one."

Dishes rattled as her mother clumsily dropped the one in her hand atop another on the counter. "What do you mean by different, June-bug?"

"You're Orson's mate, so he knew right away what he felt when you met and what it meant. But what about you? Did you know when you met him that you'd end up together?" What she didn't ask— *Did your heart race, and your entire being yearn to get closer?*

Her mother fixed her with a green gaze that Janine saw every morning when she looked in the mirror. "So many questions with complicated answers. Keep in mind ours was not a traditional courtship. When I met Orson, I was still deeply grieving and depressed about your father."

"And yet you obviously felt something? I mean, you guys did end up married after all."

"We did, but Orson had to fight hard for it." A smile stretched her mother's lips. "When he came into my life, I truly didn't think I deserved him. What your father did broke something inside me. I blamed myself."

"But it wasn't your fault."

"Says the little girl who also shouldered her own burden of guilt. We both know better now, but at the time, I couldn't help but believe I'd done something wrong. But even worse than that? The fear. I became frightened to let anybody else into my heart. I didn't want to go through the pain of losing someone I loved again. So, initially, I pushed Orson away."

"But he didn't give up." Janine remembered the flowers that arrived daily, nothing so impersonal as flower shop bouquets. Not for Orson. He picked them fresh from public gardens—and even a few backyards, he later admitted. He took Janine and her mom to dinner and movies, expecting nothing from them except companionship. Even more astonishing to a little girl, he didn't see how flawed she was. How unlovable. He came to her school concerts. Cheered at her soccer games. And when he did finally marry her mother, he did so with Janine at their side because as he claimed, "We are family."

"Orson didn't give up on me, even though I was stubborn and scared. Part of it is his tenacious nature, but a lot of that stubbornness he showed courting me was due to the fact he recognized me as his mate."

"You know I've heard that expression so many times, and yet, what does that really mean? How did he recognize you as his mate? Did he ever explain that to you? How did he know that you were the one for him?" With the barrage of questions, Janine knew she probably revealed more than she should, but who else could she ask? Certainly not Derrick, who pretended what he said was a mistake. Certainly not Orson, who would probably kill Derrick for even looking her way.

"Aren't you just a curious kitty today," her mother said with a laugh as she dropped some ice cubes into the glasses she'd poured some punch into. "Any reason why?"

"Wondering because of something I heard." She wondered if her mother caught the lie. She always did when Janine fibbed as a youngster, but if her mother did, she let it slide this time.

"You're not the only one curious. I asked Orson about it, and he said it was hard to explain. It was just something he knew. A kind of recognition by him and his bear that I was the one."

"So kind of like love at first sight?"

"In a sense, yes, except that my understanding is the mating recognition happens on a more primal level. I've done a bit of research on it, which given how closely his kind guard their secrets, wasn't easy. There are a few theories about the mating impulse. Some seem convinced it is a spiritual thing where compatible souls recognize each other and resonate, letting them know they are meant to be. Other texts say that this awareness is

148

more of an animal instinct, the predator in the shapeshifters recognizing the possibilities in breeding females."

"What do you think?"

"I think it's a combination of things. Mystical and animal."

"If you guys were so compatible, how come you never had kids?" Because if the mating instinct was driven by procreation, shouldn't that result in a fertile couple?

"We would have liked to, and it wasn't for a lack of trying." Said with a pleased grin.

"Mom! Way too much innuendo."

She laughed. "Such a prude. You asked. As you know, procreation with shifters is not always easy. Some manage it more readily than others. We weren't one of those lucky couples. But—" Her mother reached over and stroked the hair from Janine's cheek. "We never minded because we had you. Orson loves you as if you were his own. In his heart and his mind, you are his."

A soft smile tugged at Janine's lips. "I know. I know he'll never let me down." He wouldn't leave her. Just like he'd never given up on her mother. That was true love. That was a true mate. So where did that leave Derrick and his claim? Was he or wasn't he her mate? Could it be he pushed her away because he wanted to avoid tying himself to her? Given his belief he was less than a man, she wouldn't put it past him.

The real question is, what does this mean for me, for us?

She traced the granite countertop, staring at the pattern, knowing her next question would lead to possibly uncomfortable ones she wasn't ready to answer, but she had to talk to someone. "What happens if someone meets their mate, but there are obstacles keeping them apart?"

Her mother set the tray she'd prepared back on the counter. "What do you mean by obstacles? June-bug, is there something you need to tell me? Is this about that new patient of yours?"

She couldn't hold it in any longer. She had to confide. "He told me last night I was his mate. And then told me I wasn't this morning. Claimed the booze made him say it."

"That is not the type of claim his kind make lightly."

"Can you see my confusion? I know the whole mating thing is a big deal in his culture. Then again, though, his excuse is plausible. He did have a few drinks, and it was his first time out since he got back. I was thinking perhaps he made a mistake. That the excitement of the moment"—and the excitement of the kiss—"made him speak out of turn."

"I see. Let me ask you, how do you feel about this man?"

The crux of the problem. "I shouldn't feel anything at all. He's a patient. He's going through an emotionally devastating time. He needs my help. It's probably just transference."

"Except?" her mother prodded.

A heavy sigh whooshed out of Janine. "Except I feel things for him, Mom. And I know I shouldn't. I know it's wrong. So wrong. I'm his doctor. I should be above letting my emotions get involved. But I can't help myself."

"Has something happened between you?"

"Yes." She ducked her head, ashamed of her actions, but not just because she'd crossed a line in their doctor-patient relationship. The shame came from the fact that she wanted to stomp the ethical line that said she couldn't be with him.

"What are you going to do?"

Another question she had avoided answering. Janine threw up her hands in exasperation. "I don't know. The right thing would be me turning over his case. I should have done that the moment my emotions started getting involved."

"Then why not recuse yourself? Someone else can work with him. You don't have to. Perhaps some distance will give you both clarity."

Leave Derrick? Let someone else handle his volatile mood swings? Let another help him realize he had so many reasons for living? Let a stranger possibly destroy the progress she'd made and send him into a tailspin... Never. "I can't leave him. I have to see this through."

"Is this because of your father?" Her mother didn't have to specify which father she meant.

"My whole reason for working as a doctor is because of my father. But, no, my reason for wanting to stay with him is more personal than that. I care about Derrick. I don't want anything to happen to him."

"So you pity him?"

The word brought an angry retort to her lips. "Most definitely not. Derrick is strong. Stronger than he thinks. There's nothing to pity."

"Do you fear he'll do himself harm if you leave?"

Did she? "I don't think he would."

"He might if you're his mate and he thinks you've abandoned him."

Janine glared at her mother. "You're not helping here."

"Just trying to help you clarify matters. Keep in mind, you're my daughter, and you're talking about having feelings for a man who is so damaged that Orson fears he might have to take action."

"Derrick isn't a danger to anyone. He's angry at his situation, which is normal, but he's not a monster."

"Really?" Her mother arched a finely-plucked brow. "Then why are you so frightened about caring for him?"

"Other than the fact I can lose my medical license?"

Palms braced on the countertop, her mother leaned forward and caught her gaze. "Let's pretend for a moment that the whole doctor/patient thing is not an issue. Let's just say you're a woman and a man meeting for the first time. You're immediately attracted to each other. You enjoy spending time together. What is stopping you from being with him? Is it the fact he's a shifter? His infirmity? Or is it because, deep down inside, you're worried he will do to you the same thing your father did? Are you afraid he'll leave you?"

The direct questions forced her to stop and look within. She analyzed her feelings for Derrick. Attraction definitely existed between them. A simple look or touch and she was ready to melt. She wanted them to be together in a carnal sense, even though she knew he was bothered by the fact of his impotence. Yet, she didn't find herself bothered by that. She knew satisfaction could come in many ways.

Did the fact he required the use of a wheelchair disturb her? Not really, because she didn't see the chair. Sure, she understood it posed certain challenges; things that she took for granted, like going to the bathroom, were much more complicated for him. Yet…it didn't bother her. She didn't see any handicaps when she looked at him. In her eyes, he was virile and attractive. He also possessed a quick wit and a dark humor.

So why did the thought of being with him worry her? Because, now that she truly analyzed the turmoil in her heart, she couldn't help but recall a little girl who cried.

I'm scared because, at times, I see the same brewing desperation and depression I once saw in my father's eyes. Much as she might claim she didn't think Derrick would hurt or kill himself, at the same time she couldn't deny he was a man emotionally damaged. A man who could, much as she wanted to deny it, possibly hurt himself if he thought his departure would benefit others.

What if I let him into my heart and he left? She didn't think she could handle losing someone else like that.

The epiphany was interrupted by her dad entering the kitchen. She frowned as she noted Derrick wasn't with him.

"Where is he?" she asked with a hint of suspicion.

"Put the glare away. He's fine. Just visiting the powder room." Orson snagged a piece of cheese from the tray her mother had uncovered, so nonchalant while Janine burned with curiosity.

"And?" she queried. "Did you make a decision?" In other words, had her stepdad, as a shifter councilman, rendered judgment? Would Derrick live or die?

"Not exactly."

She couldn't help an impatience burst. "What does not exactly mean?"

"It means I don't know." Orson shrugged. "It's complicated. Derrick is definitely a man conflicted. But I don't think he's a threat yet. He is, however, demanding I take you off his case and that I banish him to a remote location to live out his years."

"You are not going to do that, are you?" The thought of Derrick vanishing to parts unknown brought a fluttery panic to her chest.

"I would say him leaving or not is up to him."

"He's not ready to go anywhere."

"That is your opinion. His next doctor might feel differently."

"You are not taking me off his case." She crossed her arms and adopted her most mulish expression.

"That's not up to you."

They might have argued further, but the doorbell rang as the first of the guests arrived. The next little while proved busy and chaotic, with Janine greeting friends and family who showed for the occasion.

As for Derrick, she kept an eye on him, but he didn't seem as concerned about her. After grabbing a plate of food and a drink, he disappeared. A few times, she went to hunt him down, only to have Orson intercept her.

"I was going to look for Derrick."

"He's in the billiards room with a few of my buddies shooting the shit and tossing some darts."

"I should check on him."

With a hand on her arm, Orson put a stop to that. "The man is fine. He doesn't need you hovering over him. Let him socialize. Isn't putting him in social situations part of his treatment?"

Yes, but she worried about how he handled it. In her blind haste to have Orson see Derrick as benign, she had tossed him into a situation where he might feel uncomfortable.

What if he currently hid in a corner, scowling at the world? Or someone said something and he went off the edge? What if…the guy was laughing as he threw darts from his seat, compensating for his angle and doing quite well.

Seeing him with a smile on his lips, such a rarity, she froze in the doorway. The noise would have hidden her arrival, and yet, he seemed to instantly know she stood there. He turned his head, and they shared a quick glance, quick because he turned away.

He's giving me the cold shoulder. It didn't sit well with her at all.

Then, she didn't have time to worry about Derrick because her ex-boyfriend, Brian, decided to make an appearance.

Chapter Thirteen

The tingling awareness of her presence faded as Janine moved from the doorway of the game room. He'd known she watched him. Felt her eyes on him the moment she appeared and missed her gaze when she left.

It took him gripping the wheels of his chair not to chase after her. Having her out of his line of sight didn't sit well, and not just because of all the people roaming around. Earlier, when they'd first arrived, he'd also hated sending her off into the kitchen with her mother. Then again, it was probably a good thing Red didn't stay because the first thing Derrick tried to do was get her out of his life.

"I want a new shrink."

On his way to a bar, fetching a drink of something with a fiery kick, Orson paused. "Is there a problem with my daughter?"

"No."

"Then why the request?" The council member uncorked a decanter and poured some amber liquid into glasses. He handed one to Derrick before taking a seat on the couch. "Do you want her removed because she's a woman?"

Her being a woman definitely constituted a large part of the problem. *Because she's my woman.* "I just don't think it's working out with her. I want someone else." No, he didn't. She was the only one for him, hence the reason why he had to get her far, far away. He didn't plan on telling Orson that tidbit.

Glass raised to his lips, Orson closed his eyes and inhaled. "I love the smell of a fine brandy. As a shifter, it's funny how much our sense of smell tells us. It lets us know if something is edible. If someone is a shifter. If"—he opened his eyes and fixed Derrick with a cold gaze—"someone is lying."

"I'm not lying about wanting her gone."

"No. I can see you want her out of your life, and rather desperately too. Care to explain why? Or should I guess?"

A grimace pulled Derrick's lips. "She's not safe around me."

"Not safe? Are you saying you'd harm her?"

"Never."

"Then you'd better explain yourself."

There were times a man could lie, to himself, to others, but here and now, with so much on the line, Derrick couldn't. He let out a sigh. "She's my mate, which is obviously not a good thing."

"Why not?"

Derrick couldn't help but shoot an incredulous look at the man before him. "Why not? You really have to ask?" He slammed a fist down on his dead meat snakes. "This is why."

"Are you saying my daughter is too shallow to accept you as you are?"

"No, of course not."

"Are you suicidal?"

"No, so if you're implying I would kill myself like her father did, then you can shove it. I wouldn't do that."

"Then you think you might lose control of your beast and hurt her."

"I would never harm her. Never!" Anger burned within, but it was his wolf that took the most savage exception. "Janine is bright and beautiful and caring. She deserves better than being saddled with a cripple who can't be a true mate to her. Who can never give her children. Or dance with her at a wedding."

"Shouldn't Janine be the one to make that choice?"

More was said after that, but those were the words that stuck with Derrick. The problem he struggled with most revolved around his fear if he did let her make that choice. From the moment he'd met her, he'd fought the urge to claim her. The more he got to know her, the harder it got. He kept telling himself the reason he pushed her away was for her own good but…

I'm scared. Scared that she would reject him.

If he had two legs, and a cock that didn't dangle uselessly, he would have kicked that fear to the curb, tossed Red over a shoulder, and taken her to bed until she belonged to him body, soul, and heart. But he couldn't claim her. Couldn't woo her the way he wanted to.

And he couldn't seem to get her out of his life. Orson refused to remove her as his doctor, citing, "I think she's your only chance at getting better."

Or she'd be the reason he threw himself into madness.

Knowing he couldn't seem to stem his feelings toward her led to him avoiding her as the party commenced—the only option left to him since Orson concluded Derrick wasn't a menace in need of a bullet to the brain. Or, as Orson said, "You're not Old Yeller, so stop fucking asking. You lost the use of your legs and cock, but you still have a brain, so use it."

Yeah, Derrick did have a brain, and it advised steering clear of Janine, a great plan until he noted her whipping past the door of the billiards room, looking mad, and yet it was the man following her with determination that sent him wheeling out to follow.

The home truly appeared as opulent inside as out, but with a casual comfort he could appreciate. Straight lines, relatively uncluttered rooms and halls. He took in those details as he wheeled down the hall, following the faintest hint of her scent.

At the edge of the patio doors leading outside, he paused. The doors gaped open, letting the cooler evening air waft into the house, along with the smell of flowers in bloom. It wasn't the only thing he scented.

A deep inhalation and a sifting of flavors let him know Janine had passed through here, along with someone else. He hesitated to follow. It was none of his business what Janine did in the garden. That didn't stop him from listening to the voices raised in argument.

"I told you to leave," Janine said, her words terse.

"But I just got here. I thought you'd be happy to see me." The male reply held an undertone of whining.

I hate whiners. We should tear off his head.

"We broke up, Brian."

Broke up as in they'd once dated? Now he totally wanted to rip someone to shreds.

The male scoffed. "Nonsense. We were on a break."

It hadn't worked for Ross, and it certainly didn't work for this Brian dude.

"Stop imagining something that isn't there. We are over. As in I don't want to see you. As in leave my parents' house. Now."

"Or else what?" the guy called Brian asked with evident mockery. "You're a human. It's not as if you can toss me out."

"No, but I can," Derrick growled, not content to eavesdrop in the shadows. He wheeled through the doors and made his presence known. "You heard Janine. Time for you to leave."

The blond-haired fellow spun away from Janine and arched a brow at Derrick. "Do you fucking mind? This is a private conversation. So why not take your buggy and go bother someone else?"

Red rage. Red rage. He could feel his temper rising, and with it came the wolf. He tightened his grip on the wheels of his chair.

"It's okay, Derrick." The soft green of Red's gaze met his. It somewhat dampened the anger. "I can handle this." She turned her gaze from Derrick to Brian. "Don't make this ugly. I want you to leave. We are not a couple anymore, Brian. We never will be. It's time for you to accept that and stop with the calls and texts."

"I just wanted to talk."

"Demanding to know where I am and then getting mad is not wanting to talk. It's you being a control freak, the same reason why we broke up."

Listening, Derrick clued in on one key fact. "Has this douche nozzle been harassing you?"

That got Brian's attention. "What did you call me?" He bristled, widening his chest and adopting an aggressive posture.

On the other hand, Derrick relaxed and smiled. "I called you a douche nozzle who needs to get his ass out of here now."

"Or else what?" An ugly sneer pulled at Janine's ex-boyfriend's lips. "What are you going to do, *cripple*?"

The red rage returned at the insult. "Get a little closer and I'll fucking show you," Derrick snarled. He might not be able to stand, but let him get a hold of the bastard and he'd let him talk to his fist.

"You want me, come get me." With that taunt, Brian retreated a few paces and beckoned him with his fingers.

Back in the day, Derrick would have dove on the guy and beat the shit out of him. As it was, he gripped his wheels, ready to roll into action, only to have a woman, half his fucking size, step in to protect him, emasculating him even further. "What is wrong with you threatening a war vet? You're sick, and I've had enough, Brian. You're not welcome here. So leave before I call Orson."

"You wouldn't dare, not during his anniversary party for your mother."

"Wouldn't I?" She crossed her arms and tilted her head. "What do you think he'd say if he knew you were bothering me? Or should I say, what do you think he'd do?"

Apparently, Brian had a pretty damned good idea of what would happen. Anger flashed in the other man's eyes. "I'll leave since you're obviously on your period or something, given how crabby you are. But we're not done, Janine. Not by a long shot."

"Yes, you are done. You are not to contact her again or even look in her direction. She's off-limits." Derrick shouldn't have growled the words, especially given their possessive nature. The other man, a feline shifter, even if one on the lower end of the food chain, couldn't help but catch the nuance.

"Oh ho, the plot thickens. Don't tell me this cripple is your new boyfriend." Brian laughed, the derision clear. "I see I have nothing to worry about. It's not as if this gimp can replace me in bed."

The reminder of his impotence stung, but what shocked Derrick most was Janine sliding back to stand at his side so she could cup a hand around the nape of his neck. "There's more than one way to give a woman pleasure. When it comes to satisfaction, Derrick is more of a man than you'll ever be."

The retort only served to bring ruddy color to Brian's face. "Why you fucking sl—" Brian might have said more if Orson hadn't bellowed from the doorway.

"I wouldn't finish that sentence if I were you. Get your ass out of here, Brian, before I forget who your father is!"

Apparently, Brian's belligerent courage worked only for men in wheelchairs. Against real predators, he fled, but not without tossing a dark look back at Janine and mouthing, "This isn't over."

Perhaps it was the threat to Janine that did it.

Or the fact that the douche nozzle had once laid hands on her. Whatever the reason, all Derrick knew was, when he finally fell asleep on the sofa in the den, his bed for the night, not a cuff in sight, the nightmare came with a new participant.

And when Red began to scream in his dream, he snapped.

Chapter Fourteen

Something woke Janine from a light slumber. She lay in bed, one half of her face squashed against her pillow, listening. Not even the creak of joists shifting broke the heavy silence. Holding her breath a moment longer, she tested the ambiance of the room. *Is anyone here? Am I alone?*

Her senses craned, seeking that sense of vitality that only another person could emit. She sought another presence, a reason for waking, and felt nothing. She exhaled with relief.

No bogeyman tonight.

For those who might mock her, she had no problem admitting a fear of the dark, especially the particular shade it achieved in the middle of the night. Dark deeds often happened under night's shadow. *And sometimes a little girl wakes and opens her eyes to see bloodshot ones staring right at her.* The shriek she uttered proved piercing.

The scarier thing? Daddy screamed at an even higher pitch.

But that had happened a long time ago. Only the one time, but it left an impression. She'd spent years fighting her fear of the dark. Many a night, either Orson or her mother, sometimes even both, sat on the edge of her bed and soothed her. Brushing back the hair stuck to her damp forehead and making soothing sounds and promises. Orson used to press a gentle kiss on her forehead, tuck her teddy, Ralph, under the blankets and whisper, "Never fear, June-bug. You have a bear to protect you." Orson did keep her safe, and even better, never lost himself.

But could she say the same about Derrick?

Don't start thinking about him. Go back to sleep. Easier said than done. Clamping her eyes shut did not do a thing to relax her. Sigh. The problem with getting woken with an adrenalized jolt was winding back down.

Restless, she rolled onto her back and starred at the popcorn ceiling, finding comfort in the familiar ridges. Throughout the rest of the house, her parents had scraped the ceilings smooth, except in this room at her request. When sleep eluded her, she fought her fears and relaxed by searching the shadowy shapes and turning them into something pleasant—like a bunny hopping through a field. Or, look, there was pirate ship, coasting the waves. She shifted in bed, and the shadows moved, and there was a rugged jaw. The broad shoulders much like D—

She turned away from a ceiling that seemed determined to make her think about the one thing she kept trying to avoid.

Tried being the key word.

The man wouldn't leave her thoughts. Derrick. Derrick. Derrick. Almost an obsession, one she kept trying to fight.

Get out of my head. She punched her pillow. Frustration coiled hotly inside her—especially between her legs, as she went thinking about him again. Why did he have to plague her so much? It seemed as if her ability to compartmentalize her patients from her personal life just kept failing with him. Her unorthodox ways led to maverick emotions. A part of her wanted to buck all rules and conventions to make her own choices.

Craziness, which was why she stared at the ceiling, fists clenched at her sides atop the comforter. So much for sleep. Then again, the fact that she'd slept at all proved a surprise. She'd tumbled into her bed just after one, as her parents waved off the last guests—her Aunt Minnie and Uncle Sherman, who couldn't leave an open bottle of scotch. But once that last drop was gone? So long and see you next time.

As Janine had passed the closed door to the den on the main floor on the way to the stairs for the second floor, she stared, almost hard enough surely to bore a hole through the wood. She couldn't help it, not with a few glasses of mom's punch and the knowledge Derrick slept behind the flimsy portal.

Or did he?

Did he enjoy the oblivion of a deep sleep, or did he stare at the ceiling too?

Why did she even wonder?

Because I can't help myself. With Derrick, she wanted to break all the rules. For him, she was willing to risk it all.

Madness. Derrick was a man troubled. A guy who had begun to open his eyes to the possibilities of a future and yet still resisted. Add to that he seemed a man determined to avoid her. Look at how he'd come to her rescue, only to disappear after the incident with Brian. He didn't even say goodnight.

Is he mad at me? Jealous... She couldn't help but wonder. She'd seen his face when he realized she and Brian had once been intimate. Janine wasn't so coy as to mistake the tight-lipped countenance of a man in the throes of jealousy.

He cared, yet what must he think of her? Admitting she used to date Brian must have thrown him for a loop. Janine could admit a certain guilty pleasure in Derrick's disdain for Brian, his eloquently evocative nickname douche nozzle truly an apt descriptor of her ex. Witty comebacks, however, couldn't compare to the cruel way Brian rubbed Derrick's pride by reminding him of his issue below the waist.

A low blow to a man struggling so hard to cope with losing what he felt defined his masculinity.

Did he avoid her for any of those reasons, or was there yet another?

Ever since Janine's talk with her mother, she'd wanted to have a serious chat with Derrick. *I want to ask him if he really thinks he's my mate.* Did he truly believe Janine was the one for him?

The idea thrilled—and terrified. If he did think her his mate, should she try and dissuade him of his belief or rejoice in it?

A faint noise caught her attention, a sound that didn't belong in the house she knew so well. She snapped her attention and listened for a repeat. It didn't reoccur, yet she still swung her legs out of the bed, letting her feet flatten on the cold parquet floor. Another thing she insisted they keep when they renovated every other inch of the house. She liked the patterns inside the squares.

She eschewed slippers and even a robe as she

eased across the room, moving by familiar rote away from the squeaky spots. While a good girl now, she'd more than once snuck downstairs as a teen with a bobbing flashlight, guided by the nightlights her parents put in for her, usually for a midnight snack.

Down the steps she eased, ninja-quiet in a pink nightgown that went to mid-thigh with a cartoon kitty on her chest. The house loomed around her, a familiar space changed by shadows and darkness. In the deep of night, at the witching hour of three, it was hard not to hesitate and wonder what might hide, ready to pounce. Her heart thumped, a hard, fast tempo, yet her breath barely whispered past her lips as she held tightly to it lest the noise mask more nefarious sounds.

Admit it. A part of me is wondering if Derrick sleepwalks too, rolling the halls, ready to make me pee my panties. It would take only a minute to check.

Reaching the den, she paused outside the closed door. More than likely, he rested within.

I should peek to make sure he's in there. Yet, rushing in might prove startling, especially if Derrick lay awake. Perhaps it was not even him making the noise at all.

Perhaps…

A frown drew her brows together as she stared at the solid wood paneling of the door. She couldn't help but recall Derrick remained unfettered this night.

Not his idea. According to her father, Derrick asked for cuffs, but Orson refused him. Said if Derrick planned to live on his own, he needed to start taking responsibility for himself.

On that she and her dad agreed. Derrick needed to trust that he could control his wolf. She knew he could. Hoped. Because if he didn't and he went feral in her parents' house…

No. That didn't even bear thinking. She shook her head free of pessimism and leaned forward enough that she could press her ear against the cool flat panel of the door. Breathing shallowly, she kept eyes wide open to watch the hall in front of her while worrying about what might creep from the wall behind.

Don't think about it.

Don't think about the fact that her mother had once upon a time done a walk of her own in the middle of the night, only to find—

Before Janine could let her mind go in that direction, she grasped the knob of the door and threw it open, needing to prove to herself that Derrick simply slept.

Light, glowing from a soft bulb plugged in the wall, took some of the eeriness from the room and illuminated the man lying under a thick blue comforter on the pullout couch.

He's not dead.

Of course not. Derrick wasn't her father. *He wouldn't leave me like that.*

How she wished these odd certainties would stop. They didn't help her frame of mind. Seeing him resting and looking so peaceful, his usual lines of wariness worn smooth, she chastised herself. What if she'd woken him? She knew how he usually suffered from nightmares. For once, the man slept and—

He stirred, shifting under the covers, a

grimace pulling at his features.

"No." The word whispered from his lips.

Did he talk to her, or did he dream? Before anyone could hear him, she shut the door with a quiet click. He didn't waken, his body shifting under the covers.

A step, then another, brought her to his bedside. She stared down at him and noted the rapid flutter of his orbs under eyelids.

"No. Leave her alone."

Leave who? Who did he speak of? She didn't recall hearing of any women being part of his capture and torture.

"Don't touch her. I said. *Don't. Touch. Her.*" The words emerged in a low growl, rumbled and vicious. She also couldn't miss the fact that his features took on an inhuman cast.

"Derrick?" She uttered his name softly, not wanting to startle him.

Grrrr. The low sound vibrated as it rolled from a peeled lip, baring sharp teeth. The wolf tried to rise, and Derrick, still asleep, hadn't the slightest clue.

A shiver pimpled her skin. "Derrick, you have to wake up." Because if he went loup in her father's house, who knew what Orson would do to protect her and her mother.

Another sound emerged from Derrick, a low rumble as his head thrashed from side to side.

"You have to stay in control," she muttered. Before Janine could question her actions, she clambered onto the bed and straddled his waist. He probably didn't feel her holding his lower body down with hers, but he couldn't miss the fact that she grabbed both his wrists. She might not have the strength to hold him, but she hoped to wake him before he truly got out of control.

He remained asleep, despite her maneuvering.

"Derrick." Holding his hands pinned to the bed, she leaned forward, wanting him to see her if he woke and not a strange room that might make him panic further.

His upper body undulated. Bared to the waist, she couldn't help but feel how the flesh of his chest burned hot. He thrashed under her, his frame twisting, his features contorting. Coarse hairs pushed against the flesh of her hands where she still held his wrists, a freaky sensation, yet still she held on.

"I won't let you go. I won't let you lose this fight," she muttered as she tightened her grip. "I'm here, Derrick. You're not in danger. Not anymore."

"Red." The word burst from his lips on a cry that started out soft but grew in tenor.

Only one way to stop that sound from reaching a peak and waking her parents.

Janine mashed her mouth to his, swallowing his cry. It halted the sound dead. So dead, he even stopped breathing. His lashes fluttered.

Staring into his brown eyes, she could see the wariness—and the flat shine of his *other*. She pulled her lips away with a tremulously spoken, "Derrick?"

"What are you doing?"

Being wildly inappropriate? Oh and not currently caring. "You were having a nightmare."

"And? You know I have those every night. What were you thinking coming in here, especially with me loose? I could have killed you."

"You wouldn't kill me." She'd stake her life on it.

"Yes, I could have, especially given you were mauling me in my sleep."

"Maul? I was kissing you."

His brow pulled into a frown. "Kissing me why?"

"You were going to scream."

"Wouldn't you if someone was pinning you to a bed? I probably thought you were the bogeyman come to get me."

Her turn to frown at him. "Stop twisting this around. You had no idea I was kissing you. Just like I bet you don't remember talking in your sleep."

"Big deal. I had a nightmare. I get those every night. You should know. We've talked about them." He rolled his eyes.

"Yes we did." In great detail, almost as if he relished telling her the gory parts in the hopes of chasing her away. She wasn't that easy to chase. "And never once in all the talks we had"—around the pool as she quick-walked beside him on the grounds or in the gym as he pumped iron—"did you ever mention anything about a woman being in there with you."

"There was no woman."

"That's what you said, and yet, just now, there was one in your dream. You kept asking them not to touch her. It seemed really important. Why haven't you told me about it? Who was the woman?" She had a feeling she knew, but, at the same time, feared she saw something only because she wanted it.

"There was no woman." Flatly said and with

eyes averted.

She released his hands and leaned up, only so she could grab his cheeks. "Who. Was. She. Who did you not want them to touch?"

For a moment, he fought her, silently and without movement. He fought by not answering and by keeping his gaze locked away from her.

Not this time. Not at the witching hour when boundaries were lowered and truths could be revealed. "Tell me, Derrick. Please."

At the plea, he groaned and closed his eyes. "Why can't you leave me alone?" he whispered.

"Because I can't. I just can't."

He sighed. "I wish you would. Maybe then I could escape you. But everywhere I look, I see you. Even when I close my eyes, there you are. And tonight, you made it to my nightmare."

"You thought they captured me?"

He nodded.

"But more than that, they wanted to hurt me in front of you?"

No nod this time, but she could tell by the tenseness of his frame she'd guessed true, and the thought of it pained him.

"It wasn't real, Derrick."

"Maybe not, and yet the emotions, the heart-stopping terror and rage-inducing madness of it still thunder through my veins." His eyes flashed opened and flared golden, the animal still simmering beneath the surface. "The beast wanted to kill the men in my dream. Rend them limb from limb for daring to harm you. I still do. I want to hurt something." The sentence squeezed through clenched teeth.

She let her thumbs stroke his cheeks as she

stared, hoping that, like on other occasions, she could calm the wild beast. "I'm not hurt, and you're free now."

"I wouldn't exactly say that."

"The rehab center is only temporary."

"I wasn't talking about that. I'll never be free."

"The only chains holding you down are doubt and pessimism."

"Don't you dare pep-talk me at this time of the night while straddling me only in a nightie. I might be impotent, but I'm not dead, and I'm not in the mood."

She squirmed atop him. "Are you sure of that?" She didn't miss the catch of his breath.

"What are you doing? You know I can't feel that."

"Liar. A part of you feels it, maybe not on the same physical level, but you do feel. Don't forget. You can also see." Blame her own adrenaline for fueling her boldness. She sat straight on him and grabbed the hem of her nightgown. She tugged at it.

"What are you doing?" The words emerged almost trembling. "Red, stop it. Don't you dare."

"Dare what? Take off my clothes and prove you can feel?"

His hands grabbed at hers, stopping their ascent. "You don't have to pity strip for me. I already know that I can get horny. So leave the clothes on."

"How many times do I have to tell you I don't feel sorry for you? As a matter of fact, if anyone deserves pity here, it's me. Ever since I met you, I've wanted you to touch me. Wanted to touch you in return." She pulled her left hand free and pressed it against his flesh, the heat of it a brand on her skin.

He sucked in a breath. "What happened to doctor/patient boundaries? Weren't you the one saying we needed some?"

"I can't have any boundaries from you. I tried. It just hasn't worked." The admission spilled free. "And besides, you told my dad to fire me."

"Did he?"

"Doesn't matter because I quit." She leaned down and kissed him, not because she wanted to quiet him this time, but because she wanted the taste of him on her lips.

He didn't protest any further. He caved completely to her sensual seduction. His arms wrapped around her, the strength in them great and yet gentle. Just like his kiss proved gentle, restrained.

She didn't feel the same need. She gripped his cheeks and held him for plundering. She sucked and nibbled at his lips, feeling liquid heat coursing through her veins as arousal lit every nerve she had.

With just a kiss—A kiss!—he managed to arouse her like no other. When his hands did finally start to roam, lifting the fabric of the nightgown as he skimmed her skin, he lit a path of fiery awareness.

He kept lifting the gown, and she raised herself upright, grasping the hem to pull it off completely. She wore only panties underneath; her breasts hung a little with weight, but he didn't seem to mind their lushness because his eyes flared with hunger.

Before his avid gaze, her nipples hardened into tight points, a temptation he couldn't resist. His hands rose to cup her breasts. A thumb brushed over each peak, and a shiver zipped through her.

"You are so fucking beautiful." The whispered words held such a note of reverence. And he proved his words with worship, tensing his stomach to bring his torso up and then leaning forward as he placed a hand on her nape and arched her back. He positioned her that he might lean forward and capture the tip of her breast in his mouth.

At the first wet tug, she cried out. Her head tilted and her lips parted as she closed her eyes, enjoying the blissful sensation of his lips on her breast. He paid homage to her body with his lips and tongue, even his hands.

The pleasure proved exquisite. She couldn't help but rock on him, grinding herself against him, putting pressure on her clit. She pushed back against him, her position not allowing her to touch him as she'd like.

Her turn to lean forward and latch her lips to a nipple. He hummed an appreciative note as she sucked and bit down on him. A fine tremble went through him. She squirmed in reply.

A rake of her nails down his chest brought a gasp from his lips, but he got her back by flipping her on the sofa bed—*creak*. The furniture didn't collapse, and with a chuckle, Derrick draped himself partially over her.

"I wasn't done," she said as she twined her arms around his neck to draw him near.

His lips brushed hers softly. "Neither was I."

He captured her mouth at the same time his fingers crossed the boundary of her panties. As his tongue insinuated itself to tease and please, so did his finger find her damp folds and part them.

The honey of her arousal eased his way, and he dipped his finger a few times before adding a second. Her channel clutched at his digits, and she rocked her hips as he thrust them slowly in and out. But it was when he managed to have his thumb tap at her clit that she couldn't help but clutch at his shoulders and utter a sound that his lips muffled. The very fact that she couldn't scream as her body craved sent a shudder through her.

And then another as he added a third finger to really make it tight while his thumb kept teasing her button.

It was enough to drive any woman wild. But Derrick wasn't done. He pushed himself away from her lips and settled himself between her legs. He raised her thighs so they sat on his shoulders, and his hands gripped her full cheeks, tugging her closer. The warmth of his breath tickled her nether lips.

She clutched at the sheet and clenched her jaw, the anticipation of pleasure making her glisten and tremble.

He didn't immediately lick. Instead, his fingers returned to slowly penetrate. His mouth brushed against the vulnerable skin of her inner thigh. She sighed.

He moved closer, the heat of his breath scorching. She squirmed.

"Be still," he whispered, hot against her lower lips. "Don't make a sound."

And she hoped she didn't, but she couldn't be sure because when his tongue began to lash her clit, she kind of lost it.

Chapter Fifteen

The feel of her on his fingers proved exhilarating, but it couldn't compare to her intoxicating taste. A man parched, Derrick lapped at her, savoring her womanly cream and humming with pure male satisfaction at how she clenched and pushed against him, her body craving more of his touch.

He couldn't have stopped if he wanted to. Too long he'd craved her. Too long he'd denied the unmistakable truth.

Janine is mine. And for this moment at least, he couldn't find the strength to push her away. *I'm tired of fighting what I want.* Time for a little selfishness. He lapped at her sweet button, feeling it swell at his flicks. He pumped his fingers in and out of the moistness of her sex, loving how she gripped him tight.

Her excitement built, reaching a crescendo, and he felt just as coiled as her, poised on the edge. He pistoned his fingers in her as his lips pinched her swollen button. A low cry began to keen from her lips. She smashed a pillow over her face as her body arched off the bed. Even with her last-minute muffler, he could hear her deep groans, but better than hearing the enjoyment, he felt it. Felt just how hard she came on his fingers, crushing him tight. Tasted the spice of her orgasm, an explosion of flavor that brought shudders to his frame.

Fuck me. I think I kind of came. An unexpected side effect, which, while not like the euphoria of actual fucking, left him feeling more sated than before.

Easing carefully around her splayed limbs, he inched upwards on the bed, careful with where he placed his hands to draw himself in line with her.

She didn't move. Her eyes remained shut, her lips slightly parted as she fought to recapture her breath. A greedy gaze, his of course, traced the lines of her skin still flushed with passion. Before her flesh could pimple with a chill, he drew the sheets they'd pushed aside over them both. He drew her in to him, relishing the skin-to-skin feel. He might not know what tomorrow would bring, but right here, right now, he wanted to pretend.

I want to make believe that everything is all right.

"How was it?" she asked with the most uncertainty he'd ever heard from her.

It surprised him she had to ask. He hugged her close and kissed the top of her head. "More amazing than I could have imagined." Especially since, even though he'd not given her a mating bite, a connection existed between them. He could feel it like a slender thread joining them together.

"I really should go back to my bed before my parents get up."

At her words, his arms tightened around her. "Stay for just a few minutes. Let me hold you." Fuck pride. He begged for just a little while longer. If he had his way, he'd hold her forever.

Of course her dad had lots to say about their snuggle fest. Then again, what father would appreciate finding his naked daughter wrapped around a man under his roof?"

"What the hell is going on here, June-bug?" The low voice of a father trying hard to control an explosive rage.

Someone dares sneak up on us! His wolf bristled, but Derrick kept it caged. Although he could understand the indignity of being startled. He blamed the first dreamless sleep since his injury for missing Orson's entry into the room. He quickly sat up and kept a wary eye on the bristling bear.

"Morning, sir." Best to fall back on respectful military ways, given how Orson caught him.

Having also awoken, Janine tried a feeble, "It's not what it looks like."

A brow arched into the stratosphere. "You are, from what I can tell, quite undressed, under the covers, snuggling your patient. I'd say there's only one thing to think."

Orson kindly didn't mention the fact that what they'd done probably perfumed the air. Sex, especially the oral kind, required a shower and a toothbrush to cleanse away the scent. And poor Janine, with hair tousled and gorgeous where it tumbled over her shoulders, was sporting a look no father ever wanted to see. It probably explained the low, rumbling growl.

A deep blush stained her cheeks as Janine still tried to salvage the embarrassing situation. "Derrick was having a nightmare, and I calmed him."

"Do you always calm your patients naked in bed?" rumbled her dad. "You crossed a line, June-bug. A big one, and under my roof! What were you thinking?"

At the harsh rebuke, she wilted. Inside, his

wolf paced, but that wasn't what made Derrick bristle. "Don't speak to her like that." He would tolerate no disrespect to his woman. Not even from her father.

"I'll speak to my daughter any which way I like, soldier. Just like I will handle this matter in a way I choose, given this is my home. A home, I might remind, you were invited into, but nowhere in that invitation did I grant you permission to seduce my daughter."

"First off, you don't get to decide who seduces me. And second..." Her chin tilted. "He didn't seduce me. I was the one who made the first move." Janine took blame for what had happened, and while his male side might have usually complained, in this case, his ego inflated instead.

Because I was the man.

"It doesn't matter who started it or not. The fact is it shouldn't have happened."

"I'd say the concern about what occurred is between me and Janine." It would only ever be him and Janine. A rare optimism gave him the courage to wonder if they could find a way to make things work. Forget could. He would make it work. He'd make it his new mission in life. Other people went on after grave tragedies and ailments. They did it, and by damn, so could he. But there was an obstacle in his way, and it wasn't one he could kill.

With his brows beetled, Orson glared. "You will keep your hands off her. *Or else.* And for the love of God, put something on, June-bug." Orson removed his robe and tossed it at Janine, his T-shirt and plaid bottoms keeping him respectable.

"Threatening a man in a wheelchair?"

Derrick couldn't help but sneer. A male challenged either bared his belly or challenged back.

"I don't care if you're in a full-body cast. You are not ready yet to commit yourself, and I am not convinced you ever will be. Janine has already suffered from losing one man who couldn't conquer his demons. I won't have you or anyone else hurting my daughter."

"I would never hurt her."

"Won't you? You don't just have the mental problems to deal with. I know about the shard in your back. The one the doctor says has to come out. Have you told her just how bad it is? Did you let her know that if the wolf does manage to take over, whether on accident or purpose, that piece of metal in your back has a good chance of killing you?"

Derrick's lips tightened, and he could have howled when he saw the pain in Janine's eyes. "There's an operation I can have." An operation he'd been denying, but he didn't mention that.

"I know all about the shard and the operation," Janine said, interrupting their staring game. "How could I have forgotten?" The last she said in a whisper, as if to herself. Features ashen, she turned her back to him before letting the sheet fall so she could thread her arms in the robe.

"Don't leave yet. We need to talk." Panic fluttered in his chest as he realized she would leave.

Orson snorted. "Now he wants to talk? Talk about the fact you've got no future prospect, not with that bomb in your back. I'd say you should have thought about the fact you could die and break her heart before you took advantage of her," snapped Orson.

At that rebuke, Janine's head snapped up. "Don't get mad at him. I knew full well what I was doing." She pulled the belt of the robe tight. "And I know what I have to do. Get ready. We'll leave within the next hour." She tossed that instruction at Derrick.

"You're not leaving with him." Orson crossed his arms and shook his head.

"I am. He needs me to take him back the rehab center."

"I'll get someone else to do it."

She leaned up on tiptoe and kissed Orson's cheek. "I'll be fine. You're overreacting. Derrick has never hurt me, and despite what you think, he never would. He's a good man."

Words that warmed Derrick's heart, even as part of it quivered in cold, as she wouldn't meet his gaze.

"Harrumph," was the councilor's reply as his daughter slipped past. Orson turned to watch her leave and didn't face Derrick again until they heard her steps reach the top of the stairs.

"She's my mate," Derrick said in the silence that stretched.

A piercing gaze met his. "Maybe, but Junebug deserves better than a man who still hasn't made up his mind whether he's going to live or die."

"I intend to live." Live because the world didn't seem so bleak anymore, but judging by Janine's lack of smile, she didn't quite agree.

The drive back to the rehab center was spent in stilted silence. Him brooding because of everything that had happened—including the realization it was time to get the surgery the doctor ordered—her because she probably regretted what happened.

No she didn't.

The certainty came from within. How odd. While determined to try and be the man she needed, a part of him remained convinced he couldn't give her the life she deserved.

Yeah we can.

Again with the contradiction. *Hey, you furball, stop arguing with me.* Except it wasn't his wolf causing a ruckus. *She likes me.* He could lie to himself all he wanted, such as the lie that he couldn't offer her the pleasure she deserved. He proved that wrong last night.

I proved I could satisfy. I made her come so hard there were tears in her eyes. Don't forget she clung to me all night. Hugged him tight to her body, and he enjoyed the skin-to-skin contact. Enjoyed having her close.

Wouldn't she love to hear him admit she'd been right? Perhaps he didn't sink a cock into her, but he touched and tasted her in intimate ways that proved very arousing. *No creamy spurts and yet I came.* Phantom cum, with no cleanup.

How he wanted to enjoy that delight again. If only she were talking to him, but then again, he wasn't talking to her. Because he was a stubborn ass who, despite his bravado, now found himself letting her stepdad's words send him fleeing yellow-belly style.

Is this how I want to live out my life? Tail tucked like a coward? He hadn't survived the war to get taken down by pride. "I'm sorry we got caught by your father."

"No you're not. You're not really bothered

by it at all."

He shrugged. "It was embarrassing, but not the end of the world."

"How about the end of my career?" She banged the steering wheel. "I completely smashed all my professional boundaries last night. I let myself get too close to you."

The bitter him would have said something caustic such as "*You deserve better than me.*" Instead, he said, "Of course you got close to me. You're my mate. Mine. It's only natural you feel drawn and unable to help yourself."

"Arrogant much?"

"It's not arrogance to state the truth. You and I are meant to be." The more he claimed that belief, the more certain it felt. The more he believed it.

"What happened to that speech about me deserving better?"

A chuckle rolled from his lips. "Oh, you probably deserve better. I won't argue that point, but it seems you're stuck with me."

"You seem to assume I want to be stuck with you."

"You do." How easily the old cocky confidence returned when he gave it a chance.

"Declaring it doesn't make it real."

"Arguing about it won't change it either," Derrick stated. "Trust me, I know. I've been fighting it since I met you. But do you know what I'm finally realizing? A man can only fight so many battles. In some, he needs to concede or come to grips. Where you're concerned, I'm done fighting the one thing that makes me happy these days."

"I can't be the only thing that makes you happy. That's too much expectation and pressure to put on anyone."

"If you'd let me finish, I would add that your constant reminders that life is still worth exploring have made me see some things in a more positive light."

"Such as? Because last I heard, everything sucked. Your words, not mine."

"I'm not going to lie. A lot of things still do, but there are some things that don't. Like food, for instance. Just because the rehab center food is bland, it doesn't mean I can't drool again. I mean, those chicken wings the other night were fucking awesome."

"So you're going to create your own happiness by eating good food? Sounds like a recipe for heart disease."

"This isn't just about food. It's only one example of things I've realized still give me pleasure. There's also the fact that just because I can't run doesn't mean I can't play basketball. Turns out I'm a great shot even sitting down. And I can still lift weights. I can actually do tons of shit." Even make love to a woman. "You taught me that I was more capable than I thought."

"So you're grateful to me. That's understandable, as is a desire on your part to thank me."

"I think I thanked you rather well." He couldn't help the low drawl.

A pink hue highlighted her cheeks. "Please don't talk about last night. It shouldn't have happened. I take full blame for seducing you."

A smirk tugged at his lips. "Taking blame for a seduction that was inevitable? Sorry, Red, but one way or another, what happened last night was fated. We are meant to be together."

Her head shook. "You are not ready for that kind of commitment."

"Actually, I am. I'm even ready to give you half my closet. When I get one. I don't suppose before you quit being my doc you could give me a clearance report saying I'm fit to leave the rehab center?"

She shot him a look. "You actually think you're ready to go?"

"Damned straight I do."

He could almost see the devious gears in her mind whirring before she said, "If you're ready, then you won't mind a little test."

"Bring it. I'll show you I can handle anything you throw at me."

Arrogant words he could have swallowed later when he finally faced her test. He should note he didn't have the slightest clue what she planned when she dropped him off at the rehab center, claiming she'd see him later, and she meant later as in the next day right after lunch.

The fact he'd not seen her at all since their return meant he snapped more than his fair share, but good news, that night, when the nightmares hit and threatened her, he knew enough to snap himself awake, with the reminder it wasn't real. Alone in his bed, untied he might add, he took control of his slumber for the first time in a long while.

He could do this. He had to stop letting his demons win. He would prove not only to himself, but also to Janine, that she could trust him. He, not the wolf, controlled the man. However, it was the man who chafed before this discovery when she refused to see him that night, their brief phone call going along the lines of, "I want to see you."

"We can't. Not here."

"Then where and when?" Surely she burned with the same impatience.

"I don't know."

"Don't make me come over there." Derrick knew exactly which window belonged to her. He stared at it, the vertical blinds only hinting at light, wondering, if she peeked out, whether she would see him perched under the shadowy boughs of a tree.

A heavy sigh came through the receiver, the phone he'd bargained for pressed against his ear. "Tomorrow. After the test. We'll talk and figure things out."

Ah yes, her little test. He'd pass it with flying colors.

Around midafternoon, Red finally arrived at his room, not to strip or straddle him so he could continue rediscovering the joys of sex, but to arch a brow and ask, "Are you ready to prove yourself?"

"Anytime you like, Red." The husky innuendo only made her clamp her lips.

"Let's go then."

Derrick followed as she led him to the main floor and strode with quick paces toward the common area.

What surprise did she have planned? Macaroni necklaces? A rousing game of chess? He slowed his rolling approach at the sound of many people talking.

Within, his wolf whined.

He cast her a glance. "What have you done?"

"You said you would prove you're ready."

"This isn't what I'd call a little test," he groused.

Janine smirked at him. "Chickening out?"

"Not on your life." Brave words, and yet, he hesitated before the doorway to the recreation room, currently crowded with way too many people.

People he knew.

His family, and they all knew to the second when he appeared.

Too many eyes pivoted to stare at Derrick. He stared back. No one moved. A Grayson family stand-off. What were the chances it would devolve into a brawl?

Pretty good actually, if he knew his family.

Trust his mother to break the stalemate with a loving harangue. "Derrick Jeremiah Grayson, how dare you refuse to see or talk to me." Then she burst into tears.

His mother cried, such a rare thing that Derrick wanted to beat himself up for at being the cause.

At his mother's tears, his father scowled. "Look what you did." Gruff words, and yet, there was moisture in his dad's eyes too. More than a few sets of eyes were damp, including his own—damned dusty place.

Only Naomi didn't shed a tear. She planted her hands on her hips and snapped, "You're the worst big brother ever. And a worse uncle. Do you realize you missed the twins' birthday as well as mine? You know how much I like presents."

"You're almost thirty. Aren't you getting too old for gifts?" Derrick retorted.

At her side, Naomi's mates, Javier and Ethan, winced.

Actually, more than a few people winced. His sister's eyes narrowed, and Derrick gripped his wheels, ready to flee her wrath.

But she didn't start throwing things—or random bodies—at him. His sister tossed her head and angled her chin. "I know what you're trying to do, and it won't work. I'm much more mature now that I'm married and a mother. But maturity doesn't mean I don't expect something on my birthday."

"What about Christmas?"

Her lips pursed. "That goes without saying and stop distracting me with promises of gifts. I wasn't done telling you what a jerk you are for not coming to visit."

Derrick shrugged. "I was kind of busy getting treatment."

"Did you forget how to use a phone?"

"Or text."

His family bugged him, like they'd bugged him his whole life, giving him a hard time. His brother Chris slugged him in the arm. Stu gripped the back of his chair and suddenly popped it into a wheelie and then scooted the chair forward, making engine noises.

"What the hell are you doing, fucktard?" Derrick snapped. "I'm a wounded veteran. Show a little respect."

"Respect?" Stu jolted the chair down and snorted. "Big demand from the dude who kept us shut away."

"I should have kept you there," he grumbled, but not in anger. It felt better than expected to see his family again—even if the dust in this room was killer on his eyes.

I wonder if the fact I didn't flee screaming means I passed Red's test. It occurred to him he'd lost track of Janine during his reunion with his family. He turned his head to spot her still present, leaning against the doorjamb, cool as could be and smugly pleased he was sure. "This is all your fault, isn't it? You know, when you said you wanted to test me, I was hoping for something a little more naked." *Shock me, will you? Take that!* His words brought a blush to her cheeks and more than a few snickers.

Red crossed her arms and glared at him. "Behave or I'll find a newspaper."

"Again with the urge to smack me." He patted his lap. "Come on over here and you can hit me as much as you'd like."

"Haven't you learned you can't manipulate a psychologist?" She pushed off the doorframe. "You're just trying to get a rise out of me to try and avoid dealing with your family. It's not going to work, especially since I'm going to leave. Have fun," she sang with a wave of her fingers.

She left.

"I like that girl," his mother announced.

So do I, was his immediate thought, and if he didn't think he'd fail, he would have raced after her. However, she was right. In order to prove himself worthy of her, he had to show he was ready to face the world, starting with the hardest part, his family.

Glancing around at all the faces, he couldn't help but shake his head. "How come there are so many of you here? I mean, I knew Naomi was nearby because Red brought the babies over one day." Speaking of whom, a baby girl, who'd wiggled free from her father's arms, toddled her way over. Without even thinking, Derrick scooped Mellie into his lap and allowed the sticky hands to pat his cheeks.

"It's not that far," his brother Stu claimed.

"It's a five-hour drive," Derrick pointed out.

His dad shrugged. "I did worse than that daily when I drove the truck for a few years. Keep in mind, the whole pack of us didn't do it every day. We took turns staying a few days at a time in a house we rented a few miles from here."

"You rented a house? How long have you been coming out here?"

His mother rolled her eyes and snorted. "Since the beginning, of course."

"But I left instructions for you to stay away."

"You didn't really think we'd abandon you, did you?"

Derrick, in his misery, hadn't thought at all. His throat clogged with emotion.

"Idiot." The cuff in the back of his head by Kendrick didn't cause the tightness in his chest. Damn his family for respecting his wishes but remaining close at hand in case he needed them.

Derrick ducked to hide his stupid watering eyes. "I was having issues dealing with some stuff."

"We hadn't noticed." Naomi's sarcasm proved ripe.

"I think he was bulking up so he could try and kick our asses," Stu announced.

"And exactly how am I supposed to do

that?" The bitter retort snapped free at the first actual comment hinting at his condition. "Is this your way of pointing out the obvious?" He slammed a fist on his legs. "These don't work. At all. My days of starting brawls and winning them is over."

"Chill, dude." Stu raised his hands. "Before you get all mightily offended, first off, I wasn't talking about you getting into a fight. Check out what we brought." His brother grabbed a folded wheelchair that leaned against the wall, its bars spray painted a bright metallic blue. He snapped it open, and Derrick gaped for a moment at the backrest.

"Speedy Stu?"

His brother plopped into the seat and gripped the wheels, bouncing himself around and spinning in tight circles. "While you've been bulking up, we've been practicing."

"We?"

Three more wheelchairs popped open, red for Demonic Angel—his brother Chris—a yellow one for Kendrick labeled Killer Smile, and for Mitchell, the Green Machine.

The customized wheelchairs spun in the space while Derrick shook his head. "What have you dumbasses done now?"

Popping a tight spin, Chris grinned. "We're about to launch the first ever Grayson Indy 100."

"You want to race me?" Incredulity in his words, but a certain spot of adrenalized excitement coursed in Derrick's veins.

"Duh. We've been waiting months for a chance to test out our skills against a master."

Damn his brothers. Finding something athletic they could do that Derrick could handle.

Assholes with their mushy caring made the dust levels rise in the room again.

Naomi yanked something from her large handbag. Ratt-a-tat. She shook the can of spray paint. "So what do you think we should call dumbass? Grumpy Beast. Lazarus."

"I've got a better one." A racing name that would drive Janine mental.

Chapter Sixteen

Doctor's Pet.

She read the title in gleaming silver letters on the back of Derrick's chair as he whipped by with a whoop, well ahead of his brothers in their own colorful chariots.

When she'd come across some orderlies watching something out the window, she'd not expected to see the Grayson clan gathered out front, clapping and hollering at the participants in the wheelchair races. It wasn't even just Derrick and his brothers playing. They'd gotten several other patients to join in too.

Given the speed at which they raced, a fear for their safety made her want to march out that door and tell them to stop, but an old adage came to mind—*boys will be boys*. And men would do stupid things that resulted in stitches for, as Stu said upon meeting her, "*Shits and giggles*."

The main surgeon for the rehab center came to stand beside her. "Looks like fun," he noted.

"Yes. Dangerous, though," she added.

"These men have been to hell and back. Do you really want to mollycoddle them now?"

Yes. A part of her did. Especially since she still recalled the report analyzing Derrick's most current set of x-rays.

"This kind of exertion could shift that

fragment in Derrick's back." Heck, the exertion they'd indulged in the previous night could have killed or paralyzed him worse too. The shocking reality of it stunned her. *He could have died in my arms.*

Yet how could she deny him now? She possessed no willpower where he was concerned—she'd almost gone to him so many times the previous day while in the midst of planning this reunion. The only way to get away from the temptation and let him get the treatment he needed was to leave.

Leave before he breaks my heart.

"That shard of his won't be an issue for long. I don't know how you convinced him, but he's finally agreed to have the operation."

"He has?" She wanted to say it wasn't because of her, but that would be a lie. The only reason Derrick thought he should live and get the help he needed was because he wanted to be with her.

So utterly flattering. Yet, at the same time, terrifying. Firstly, because she didn't want the pressure of being responsible for his happiness. He needed to live first and foremost for himself.

The second reason his attachment frightened? Because he might die. She didn't just have this lingering piece of metal to worry about, but his general mindset. How strong was his will to live?

What if I do give him what he wants, what I want, and he dies? Could she handle that crushing pain?

But at the same time, what if leaving sent him off the edge? What if leaving hurt her even worse?

She wished for a clear answer, a sign, but the

God so many believed in didn't answer, much like he'd never answered a little girl's prayers to fix her daddy.

Laughter brought her attention back to the Graysons, clustered around the chairs, happy and together. She pressed her hand against the window, the twilight outside hiding how she looked longingly one last time upon Derrick.

Yes, last. She couldn't stay. Not if she wanted him to get better. The guilt she felt at leaving was now balanced by the fact that he wasn't alone anymore.

In between races, he spent the rest of that afternoon and part of the early evening outside with his family, allowing himself to sprawl on a blanket his mother procured from somewhere. Laughing as his brothers tried to replicate the ease with which he got on and off his chair.

One last look turned into many as, from a distance, Janine couldn't help but watch. She soaked in the glimpse of the old Derrick, the carefree one who forgot to scowl at the world and who thrived with the love and acceptance of his family. In that moment, he remembered happiness, a happiness that didn't need her.

And that hurt. The selfish part of her enjoyed thinking he needed her and only her. Her mindset was so freakn' twisted. *I need to get away from him.*

Before she could change her mind and do the wrong thing, she did the one thing she never advocated doing. She planned to run.

Returning to her room, she packed her bags and debated simply leaving. No one, not even a therapist, wanted to deal with the emotional wringing that would come from confronting him.

But I owe it to him to say goodbye. Even if she feared the strength of her resolve if he begged her to stay.

Staying wasn't an option, though.

The decision to avoid Derrick was taken from her as a knock at her door had her whirling. Surely it couldn't be him. They didn't allow patients into the staff quarters.

Yet, she knew who was on the other side of the door, felt it somewhere within, almost as if they shared a connection. A frightened part of her wanted to pretend no one was home and hide. Sure, it lacked maturity, but it would be easier. But since when did she take the easy path?

Act like an adult. You owe it to him to say goodbye. She swung open the door to her quarters and stepped back. "Come in."

Derrick wheeled himself in, and his keen gaze immediately went to the packed suitcase with her sweater folded on top and her laptop bag by its side.

"Going somewhere?" Dangerously low spoken words.

"Yes." She laced her fingers together and stared at her feet, lacking the courage to face him. She no longer had her professional standing as a doctor to fall back on. Her departure didn't come about because the job was done. This was her standing in front of a man she'd grown to care for, a man she was pretty sure she loved, a man she chose to leave.

"I'm going to guess by your expression that you didn't pack to move in with me."

"Patients can't have roommates."

"Don't quote the stupid rules to me. What's going on? Why are you leaving? I thought I passed your test this afternoon. I saw my family. I acted like a big fucking crybaby with them and came here tonight to man up enough to admit you were right. I did need to see them."

"I'm glad things went so well." He'd need his family to stay the course.

"The reunion went very well, and yet here you are packing to leave. Did I miss something?"

"I am no longer the therapist assigned to your case."

His brows drew together. "I guess the fact you're not my doctor anymore means you need to find some new digs. That's cool. If you give me a few minutes, I can be packed to come with you."

"You can't leave."

"Watch me. Where you go, I go. It's part of the whole mated thing. Good or bad, we're tied to one another now."

"What if I don't want to be tied to you?" She straightened and aimed a glare his way.

"Finally, we get to the real reason you're avoiding me and acting uptight."

"I wasn't avoiding you. I was busy."

"I call bullshit. Even now you can't meet my eyes. We're connected, Red. When are you going to accept that?"

"No, we're not. We slept together."

"And you now regret it."

"No." In this, she wouldn't lie to him. She wouldn't leave him thinking he didn't satisfy her because, the truth was, he satisfied her all too well. "You made me feel things, incredible things. But we

199

can't be together, not with the danger."

"Is this about you being afraid I'll leave like your daddy?"

"Yes." Again, she wouldn't lie.

"I'm not going to kill myself."

She believed him when he said it. Believed him, and yet… "You can't promise that. I know you're having the surgery for the shard in your back. You could die on the table."

"Die, or even end up worse off than I am now." He shrugged. "I've been told there is a fifteen percent chance its removal will improve my quality of life."

"Those aren't great odds." She couldn't pretend the glass sat half full, not this time, not with Derrick.

"Nope. The odds are shit. But I'm willing to risk it, and do you know why?" He rolled closer. "Because I want to live for you."

"And if it fails?" She couldn't help the crack in her voice. Then the tightness in her throat as she whispered, "What if you die? What happens to me then? Don't you see why I can't be with you? I have to leave now before things go any further."

"It's already too late, for both of us," he snapped. "We are tied together now, Red. I tried fighting it. I wanted so badly to stay away from you so you wouldn't have to face my reality."

"It's my fault. I should have never gone to you," she muttered through a clogged throat as tears clung to her lashes.

He slammed the side of his chair, a loud bang as his frustration boiled. "Don't you dare fucking take that night away from me, Red. What happened was right. Real. You're my mate."

"Am I, or was I just willing and convenient?"

"Is that what you think?"

"I don't know what I think. My education tells me that you formed an attachment to me because of the intimacy of the therapy."

"But what does your heart say?" he asked.

"My heart says you'll break it."

With those final words, she grabbed her purse from the dresser and escaped the room. Ran away from Derrick.

Confusion swirled around in her mind, and she knew staying around him would only make it worse. She wanted him. Wanted him so badly. But before she could trust his determination to be with her too, he not only needed to survive his surgery, he also needed to spend time on his own. Needed to become independent and meet other people. Meet other women. See how they made him feel.

And then, like the little bird let out of its cage, if he truly loved her, if he truly needed her, he would return.

But she doubted that would happen. Her own daddy didn't think she was special enough to fight for.

When the elevator didn't come right away, she skipped it, had to, because Derrick wheeled down the hall with grim determination in his eyes and a bellowed, "Get your ass back here, Red."

Instead of obeying, she shoved the bar on the stairwell door and darted through. In a sense, she cheated, skipping down those steps, but to stay behind meant more talk. She couldn't handle more talk right now.

She raced across the gleaming tile floor of the front lobby, a peek over her shoulder showed the elevator sitting at her floor. She didn't have long to escape. Derrick would quickly catch her once he hit the ground level.

Through the glass doors, she shoved—the doors meant to keep people out, not in. She ignored the cement and paved paths of the rehab center grounds in favor of cutting across the lush green lawn, using every dirty advantage she could think of.

The parking lot loomed ahead of her, the lights that usually illuminated it dark. Perhaps malfunctioning, she didn't really care. Enough ambient light from the buildings helped guide her among the humps of vehicles.

What the meager light didn't help, though, was her internal trepidation. Anxiety coiled within at the strange darkness and shadows. Logically, she knew ghosts didn't exist, and that zombies—ones wearing the uniform her father was buried in— wouldn't pop out to frighten her, or eat her brains.

Logic, though, had nothing on irrational fear. As she had every day for over twenty years, she refused to let that fear rule her. Head held high, she strutted at a fast pace and kept an ear tuned for signs of pursuit.

She never heard or expected the arm that shot from the darkness and clotheslined her.

Wham.

The solid length hit her in the chest, and she lost her balance, slamming her onto the ground. Her head snapped on impact, a sharp pain that saw her blinking up at the sky and seeing stars, real stars that found themselves blocked by a sneering countenance.

"If it isn't my cheating whore of a girlfriend. I've been waiting for you to come out."

Woozy from the fall and bump to her head, she didn't reply, but tried to roll over.

Brian was having none of that. He straddled her prone body and latched his fists onto her wrists.

"Let go of me."

"Never. You're mine, and it's about time you started respecting that."

"Like hell. Guards. Guards!" she yelled, only to cry out when he released one arm long enough to slap her.

Yet that wasn't the most shocking thing Brian did.

A nasty chuckle rolled slickly over her, giving her the most awful shiver. "Don't bother calling for help. I took care of those idiot guards already."

"You killed them?" Shock pitched her words up an octave.

"No. Merely sent them running elsewhere while I took care of business. I have to say, it was mighty kind of you to come running straight into my arms."

"You won't get away with this."

"And who's going to stop me?" As his fists remained clamped around her wrists, when he got to a kneeling position and stood, he yanked her along with him. That wasn't as worrisome as the dragging.

"Where are you taking me? Let go." She squirmed, fighting his grip, but Brian, a fit male with shifter strength, wasn't about to release his prize.

Not until someone else told him to. "Get your fucking hands off *my* woman."

At Derrick's boldly growled command, Brian stopped dragging her and whirled. A smirk twisted his lips. "If it isn't the crippled boyfriend. Come to say goodbye? Or did you want to come along for the ride and get a chance to see how a real man takes a woman?" Releasing one wrist, Brian freed a hand to fist her hair and yank her painfully close. He chuckled. "I bet I can make her scream."

"I bet I can make you scream too." Derrick pulled something from his lap, and despite her own circumstance, Janine's eyes widened at the sight of a gun. The barrel steadied, pointed at Brian, who showed no compunction about shifting her to cover him as a shield.

"Trust the cripple to bring a gun to a shifter fight."

"Release my mate." Derrick's flat tone left no room for argument, but Brian didn't heed it.

"Or else wh—"

The sharp retort of the gun startled a scream out of her and a bellow from Brian. Apparently, her ex had underestimated Derrick. A wheelchair didn't make a former army soldier defenseless, nor did he forget how to aim. Although she did wonder where and how he'd gotten a gun.

Released by a sagging Brian, she lunged forward, only to fall to the ground as her feet betrayed her.

Hearing the snarl didn't prepare her for the monster that latched onto her ankle, the teeth sharp daggers that cut through fabric and skin. It appeared, despite the gunshot, Brian wasn't quite dead, and his feline side was pissed.

"Shoot him," she cried to Derrick, unable to

free her leg.

"I can't. I only had the one fucking bullet."

"Get help," she screamed as the teeth dug deeper.

Instead of racing away, a low, rumbling sound emerged from Derrick as he *changed*. She saw the moment he lost control of his wolf. Fur sprouted, his features contorted, but before his hands became paws, he pushed himself from the chair, throwing himself at the furry body chewing on her leg.

Having his hindquarters drag didn't stop Derrick's Lycan side from viciously attacking Brian. Already weak from loss of blood due to the gunshot, the battle didn't last long, not once Derrick got a hold of Brian's feline neck and squeezed tight.

She closed her eyes, not just to avoid the feral nature of it, but because of the radiating waves of pain in her leg. Yet, she opened them quickly as claws scrabbled on asphalt and hot breath washed over her face.

The wild gaze of an animal, finally let loose, stared back. In his eyes she could see the rage, the rage of a beast caged and in pain for so long. More worrisome, she saw nothing of the man. The wolf had taken over.

The beast growled, its lip peeling back over gums to show teeth. It didn't seem too happy with her at the moment.

"Nice wolf?"

Grrrr.

She shifted her body, trying to get to her knees, only to cry out as the pain in her ankle throbbed in protest.

Whine. The wolf pawed at the ground, and she reached out to touch it.

"It's okay. A few stitches and I'm sure I'll be fine." Said with a grimace as she tried to draw her feet under her to stand.

She didn't make it, collapsing to her knees with a cry.

The evidence of her pain acted as a catalyst with Derrick. Fur receded, flesh reappeared, along with the bright gaze she'd come to love.

"Don't leave," he whispered, his arms wobbling. She never did reply to his plea, as he collapsed hard, and she heard him utter the most horrified whisper. "I can't move."

Chapter Seventeen

The hot satisfaction at having brought down the enemy paled before the panicked realization that Derrick couldn't move. Not a single damned muscle.

The cold reality sent his wolf into hiding, pulling back from the dead weight of his body and leaving only human flesh. Flesh that felt nothing but the tips of her fingers on his cheeks as she cradled his head.

"Derrick. Oh God, why did you do that?" She hugged his head, and if the moment weren't so dire, he might have enjoyed being buried against her plush tits. But all he could think was, *This is the last time.* The last time he'd smell her or feel her touch because he'd fucked up majorly in skipping the surgery and now paid the price.

Since he didn't expect he'd get another chance, he whispered, "I love you," which only caused her to rock and hug tighter.

In a voice thick with tears, she retorted, "This better not be one of those goodbye speeches. You're going to be fine. We'll get you in for that surgery, and everything will be okay. It has to be."

As her voice broke, he understood his selfishness in allowing himself to care for her because she, in turn, cared for him. *She was right about me hurting her.* He was about to leave her like her father had. He would die, and she would blame herself.

Who says I have to die? An inner voice spoke out against his pessimism. It wanted to know why he wanted to give up. He was strong. Hadn't he proven how strong? His shifter blood meant he healed so much better than a human. Add to that he now wanted to live, live with a vengeance so he could be with this woman.

"No goodbyes. I'll be okay. I do, after all, come from strong stock."

She laughed through her tears. "Yes, you do."

Strong, though, didn't mean he didn't make a plea. "Promise me you'll be there when I wake up."

"I promise to be the first person you see when you wake up."

He held tight to those words. He needed to lest the panic claw him down into a dark abyss.

The following hour was a whirlwind of lights and sound as an ambulance arrived to take him to the hospital where his doctor met them. Through it all, Janine remained by his side, a hand cupping his cheek, the only spot he could feel.

The greenness of her gaze was the last thing he saw before his lids fluttered shut, victim to the drugs being pumped into his body.

It seemed as if he only blinked, a scant second of time passing, before he opened them again, his mouth thick and his eyes gritty. In a sense, he felt as if he'd not slept at all, and yet he must have since he could tell by the white tiled ceiling he wasn't in the operating theatre any longer.

Inhaling through his nose didn't help dissipate the astringent scent of cleaners and the myriad other smells that permeated hospitals. With his sinuses failing him, he couldn't tell if he was alone.

"Red?" Her name whispered from his lips, a rusty sound that he feared got lost amidst the various beeps and whooshes of the machines on either side of him.

Yet, she must have hovered close by because he did one slow blink, and the next time he opened his eyes, Janine stood there. Her gorgeous eyes bored into his, and he could hear the concern in her voice as she said, "You made it." A relieved smile stretched her lips. "How are you feeling?"

"Dopey, and I don't mean the dwarf kind." He grimaced. "Hate drugs." Why anyone would want to dull their senses he could never grasp.

"It should wear off pretty quick. What about the, um"—she paused—"rest of you? How does it feel?"

Shit. The query reminded him why he was groggy. The operation. The last-ditch effort to make sure he didn't croak or turn in to a mannequin head, good only for apprentice barbers to do a shave on.

Did the operation succeed? Had he beat the odds?

For a moment, he found himself too afraid to try. Too terrified to attempt a twitch of his finger in case his greatest nightmare came true.

Don't be a fucking pussy. Leave that to his brother-in-law Javier and his extended family of big cats. Derrick was made of sturdier stuff—and an impatient family. Apparently, Janine didn't stand sentinel in his room alone.

"Stop screwing around and wiggle something already," Naomi snapped.

"Don't talk like that to your brother," his mother chided.

"But she's right," interjected Mitchell. "He is drawing things out."

"Attention whore," coughed Stu.

Fuck, had they crammed the entire family in his room? He craned his head—which worked, yay—and noted, yes, indeed, the room was packed, an avid audience for the hand that he lifted and projected into a middle finger salute.

A collective sigh went through the room, and he felt like sighing himself. At least he'd gotten the top half of his body working again, and he knew now that there were worse things than being paralyzed from the waist down.

But was the rest of him still broken? The surgery would have removed the metal lodged against his spine. The question they all wondered was, had his body managed to repair the damage?

Even if it cost him his mancard, he couldn't help but admit that he was too scared to find out.

His family didn't have the same trepidation. Chris snorted. "Are you going to lie there all day, or are you going to do something?"

"How do you know I'm not trying?" he snapped back.

Janine wrapped her fingers around his. "Maybe we should give Derrick some space. Sometimes, this kind of nerve damage takes time to heal itself."

Patience never was a Grayson strong suit.

"I say we see if he's still ticklish." Kendrick cracked his fingers as he moved into place at the foot of his bed.

The blanket was whipped off his lower legs, and the cooler air of the room brushed Derrick's skin. *My skin. I felt it!*

Before he could absorb that fact, his brother ran a finger down the sole of his foot, a very ticklish foot. A foot they were all watching.

So Derrick kicked Kendrick—in the face. Not a hard kick, his legs were too weak from disuse for that, but still a kick.

His brother's head snapped back, and not for the first time in his family, violence was met with cheers.

Derrick smiled. Then laughed. "Fuck me, it works." Perhaps, not as great as before, he noted as he did his best to wiggle his ten toes, his left side barely twitching, but dammit, he had some movement. He drew his hand out of Janine's and couldn't help a grope under his covers.

His brothers laughed, and his sister uttered an emphatic "Gross," but he didn't care how indiscreet his actions because he had to know if his dick had feeling too. He gave it a good tug, and his cock gave him a twitch.

Good news not just for him, but also for the woman he'd claimed as mate. A mate he no longer sensed.

He craned his head to the side, only to see the door to his room swing shut as Janine left.

She left me.

And no matter how long he waited, she didn't come back, the note she left the only goodbye.

Dear Derrick,

I kept my promise and stayed until you woke. I am

so happy that you've gotten some sensation back in your lower body. The recovery will be hard, but I know you can persevere. Unfortunately, you need to do it without me at your side. While a part of me wants to be selfish and believe you when you say I'm your mate, I can't help but wonder if you mistook gratitude for affection. I'm giving you the chance to find out.

Heal yourself, Derrick. Heal your mind. Heal your body. Find out what you really need in life to make you happy.

I wish you nothing but the best.

~~Janine~~ Red

Stupid, stubborn woman. She still thought he didn't truly want her. That she was just a convenient female body.

He'd show her how wrong she was. *I will get better, Red, and when I do, I'm freakn' coming for you.*

Chapter Eighteen

With Derrick buried in the bosom of his family, Janine slipped away before the tears blurring her gaze were noticed. Derrick had survived the surgery and seemed about to beat the odds. He would recover, which meant it was time for her to go.

Even if I love him.

And she did love him. Loved him so much that she couldn't be with him.

She knew Derrick thought himself in love with her, that she was his mate. Much as she wanted to believe that, she couldn't. He'd fallen for her only because, at the time, he depended on her. Acting as his therapist meant their close involvement brought them together and imbued him with a false sense of intimacy.

I think the intimacy came from you letting him touch you.

Acts that shouldn't have happened, and yet, she didn't regret. It made leaving so much harder, but she did it now while she could. Now while he had his family and the promise of a bright future ahead of him. Let him get on with his life. Find a woman to settle down with—sob.

With her heart shattering, this time she took the cowardly route and left him a note. A note that didn't say half of the things she felt, didn't tell him how much she'd rather stay. She didn't want to confuse him any further. She'd already done enough.

The little voice in her head, which complained she was the one hurting him by leaving, got locked into a room. Derrick could handle her departure. He'd proven he could handle anything.

As the days, then weeks, and finally a month then more went by without a word, a text, nothing, she realized she'd made the right choice. For him.

As for her, she cried every night, feeling his loss keenly. She lost weight and her smile. She threw herself into her work, but found each day dragged in a gray misery she couldn't shake.

Her parents tried to drag her out of her funk with well-meaning concern.

"June-bug, you've lost weight. Let me bake you a cake, a decadent chocolate one," from her mother.

"What the hell is wrong with you?" from Orson. Followed by, "Do you want me to dispose of him? I can, you know." A dark promise from a stepfather who loved her so much he couldn't stand to see her sad.

But she'd get over it.

Eventually.

She hoped.

In the meantime, she did have other things to deal with. The police and their investigation into her wound, as well as Brian's, led to some interesting conversations.

"So you're claiming a wild wolf attacked you?" the policeman asked.

"Yes. A great big one. Derrick scared it off." Not a complete lie.

While animal attacks were rare, especially in

settled areas, the coroner who examined Brian confirmed her story because of the teeth marks on his corpse. Despite efforts, the feral canine was never found, which sucked for Janine. Want to know what proved less pleasant than the stitches on her ankle? The rabies shots she had to suffer.

Add to that physical discomfort a strange disgruntlement, part relief, or mostly disappointment, when the full moon came and went with her remaining human. Sure, she knew the shifter gene wasn't passed on by a bite—still, though, a girl could hope. *If I was furry, too, then at least I'd belong in his world.*

The knock at her door came with a sudden briskness that caught her off guard, probably because no one should be knocking. Given her apartment resided on the seventh floor, and the building had a secured entrance, she had to wonder who mistakenly rapped. Especially since she wasn't supposed to be here. The person subletting the place had to fly out west for a family emergency, so Janine, after a few weeks at her parents', now slept in her bed.

Knock. Knock. Knock. Why did she not answer? It was probably a neighbor or—

A strange tingling spread through her body. Flesh, which only moments ago lagged with fatigue, became alive with awareness.

No. It couldn't be.

A frantic urgency made for clumsy fingers as she fumbled at the lock. Shoving the door wide, she could only gape as her numb hands dropped rather than maintaining a grip. She could only stare—with hope fluttering in her breast—as Derrick wheeled himself into her place.

He's here. Why?

"Wh-what are you doing here?" she stammered, taken aback by his unexpected appearance. Surprise didn't mean she didn't inhale him, her eyes devouring how good he looked. The broadness of his shoulders stretched his shirt, and his hair held the freshness of a cut and his jaw a recent smooth shave.

Someone hadn't suffered with her absence. "You look good," she finally said when he didn't reply.

"While you look like crap. You've lost weight. And what's up with those dark circles under your eyes?"

Her lips pulled down as he remarked on the signs she couldn't hide. "I haven't been sleeping well."

"Neither have I."

Immediately, she couldn't help but be concerned. "Are you having problems with the dreams still?"

"A little, but nothing I can't handle. My sleeping problem is a little more physical."

"Is it your legs? Has your recovery not gone well?" she asked. She had no idea about his progress, as she'd not dared to ask for reports. Much like a smoker, she decided it was best to go cold turkey. Or cold wolf. Didn't matter. She'd done her best to forget Derrick. Not very well, she might add, but the attempt had been made.

"My body is fine."

"Then what's keeping you from sleeping?"

"You're not there."

"I'm sorry I took off during a crucial moment in your treatment, but given my personal involvement—"

"You didn't leave just because you were my doctor and things got a little hot and heavy. Part of the reason why you abandoned me is because you thought I didn't need you."

"I didn't abandon you. Okay, I kind of did," she amended at his pointed glance. "But I did it for good reasons."

"I wouldn't call them good. Actually, I'd say most of them were bogus. Like the one where you thought I only cared for you because you were convenient." A buzzing sound slipped past Derrick's lips. "Wrong."

"You came all this way to tell me I was wrong?" *What about telling me you loved me and missed me and...*

"I came here to tell you a few things. One is that I conquered my nightmares. No more straps for me at night, unless you're into that kind of thing." Wink.

Her heart fluttered and she found her mouth too dry to reply as he continued.

"One thing that's really helped is they sent me some army dudes to talk to, guys like me who went through some bad shit. Turns out, they were better than a therapist, present company excluded of course." A smile *and* a wink this time.

A faint, "Of course," was her loquacious response.

"Anyhow, with their tough love, Boris, that ornery bastard giving it to me hardest, they taught me how to cope with the panic and other shit. I know now that I won't ever be able to erase what happened, but I can make sure it doesn't keep me from a future."

"I told you those things too. How come they didn't sink in?"

The boyish smile that crossed his lips almost sent her to her knees.

"You didn't threaten to tie my wheelchair to the bumper of a car and go for a ride on the highway."

"They threatened you?" She couldn't help but screech.

"You don't understand because you're a woman."

"I see they did nothing to cure you of your chauvinism."

"No, but they did cure me of a need to remain in care. I did so well with my new therapy that they released me from the rehab center two weeks ago."

Two weeks out in the real world, and he'd only now come to find her. So much for thinking he'd come running to her to make a declaration of love.

The smile she pasted probably looked as fake as her words sounded. "I knew you could do it."

"Don't pull that bullshit with me, Red. Of course I did. I had to. You didn't leave me a choice when you left."

"You did it because of me?"

"Yes, you. When you left, I realized you were right. I was too messed up for it to work. So I set out to change that."

"And succeeded by the sound of it," she said.

"Of course I did. But do you want to know the one thing I couldn't fix or change, no matter what?" He leaned forward in his chair. "I couldn't change how I felt about you. All those feelings, they're still in here." He thumped his chest.

"Then why have you waited so long to come find me?"

"Why? Because I had to prove it to myself, and to you, that what I felt was real. I don't need you because you're my doctor. I don't want you because you're convenient. I love you because you're the only one for me. I guess, the question is, Red, can you love me too?"

The words sucked the breath from her, and her vision blurred. She wanted so much to believe.

Why wouldn't I believe? The man fought all his demons to show himself worthy. How many more tasks will I give him before I accept the truth?

He loves me.

What could she say? What should she say? "I love you too. Walking away was the hardest thing I've ever done. It hurt." Her turn to hit her chest. "I hated losing you."

"Oh, Red." He stood up from the chair, and her eyes widened as he took a step toward her, one leg moving well, the other dragging. But he did it. He limped to a spot in front of her and lifted her chin with a finger. "It almost killed me to stay away. It wasn't enough to have Orson and my family watching over you. I wanted to be there too."

"You had me watched?" Some people might have screamed creepy, but she actually found herself elated. Even when she'd thought herself alone, he'd been watching over her.

"Just because I was following a certain red-headed doctor's orders about getting better didn't mean I stopped caring. I made sure you were safe while I worked on becoming whole again. I almost managed it." He thumped a leg. "The nerves on this side didn't recover too well. Doctor says this is as good as it gets. But hey, at least I'm out of the chair most of the time." His lips quirked in a half-smile.

"Don't you know, though, that I loved you no matter what?" She loved the man, not the body—although the body didn't hurt.

"Just like I loved you despite the fact you were a doctor."

"Despite?" She arched a brow.

"Okay, so maybe I can admit the fact I can call you doctor when we're both naked is exciting."

Speaking of naked... "So where do we go from here?" she asked, looking up at him, not having realized before just how tall he stood.

"Only one place to go. To bed, of course." With a declaration boldly stated on grinning lips, Derrick scooped her into his arms and made his way with a hitching gait to her bedroom. He tossed her on the bed and stood at the foot of it. She pushed herself partially up on her elbows and noted his intent gaze.

"Strip for me," he ordered. "I need to see you. I spent so many nights thinking about you, thinking about that one night we shared."

"What about you?" she asked, coming to her knees, fingers clutching the hem of her shirt. "Do I get the same kind of peek?"

"You want naked, you've got naked." His shirt went soaring, revealing his broad chest, tanned from the outdoors, the white lines of old scars bisecting it. "Your turn."

Biting her lip, out of excitement, not nervousness, she yanked her own top off and let it flutter to the floor.

"Bra too."

It unhooked in the front and joined her shirt.

A slow, sexy grin stretched his lips. "Beautiful."

"If you say so."

"Oh, I do. And I also say get those pants off."

This time, she didn't hesitate. She shucked her bottoms, but left on her panties. She arched a brow at him. "Your turn."

"Not yet. I've been waiting to touch you for so long, I'm liable to spill before I even get my cock close to you."

The heady compliment flushed her body with arousal. "And did it never occur to you I might feel the same way?" She dragged the tips of her fingers down her body, tracing a path between her breasts down to the top of her underpants.

He groaned. "Red. Why are you torturing me?"

"Because I want you. I want you holding me tight and never letting me go. I want you inside me, marking me and filling me with yourself." She didn't hold back, not when she could see the bulge at his groin.

Any other time, she might have laughed at his impatience in removing his jeans, but she couldn't mock him, not when the same urgency coursed through her veins. His briefs went the same path of the jeans, leaving him gloriously bared, the thick and long root of him jutting with impatience.

Oh my.

He came at her in a rush, naked flesh and muscle touching her skin as he flattened her on the bed. Despite his frenzy, he proved gentle, holding most of his weight off her.

But after weeks of loneliness—and a lot of frustration—she didn't want gentle. She wound her arms around his neck and pulled him to her, needing the intimacy of a kiss.

Lips met and slid with erotic flair. The tips of her breasts rubbed against his chest, turning her erect nipples into hard points. How she loved the sweet rasp of her buds teasing along his slightly furred chest. The friction proved delicious, as delicious as his kisses.

It didn't take long for them both to pant hotly, the temperature of their bodies feverish with lust. Every touch, every kiss, every sensual slide of skin only served to raise her fever.

And he seemed intent on driving her mad with pleasure as his head dipped that he might grasp a nipple with his lips and tug.

"Derrick!" She gasped his name as her fingers threaded his hair. She groaned and arched her back as he suckled at her breast, the suction a direct tug to something wicked and erotic between her legs.

All of her burned for him. Burned with need. And only he could quench it. She had the dead batteries in her trash can to prove it.

"I need you," she managed to say between moans of pleasure. "Please. I need you now."

He captured her pleas with his mouth as he rose over her, bracing his weight with his hands and arms on either side of her body. Her legs spread wide to accommodate the width of him. The head of his cock brushed against her sex and drew a long moan. Lips busy kissing, he relied on his dick to find its way between her nether lips, parting them and pressing against the opening of her sex.

Big. Very big.

"Thank you," he rumbled.

Oops. She'd said that out loud. But she only spoke the truth, and the truth was she wanted him to sink inside her. She wrapped her legs around his flanks, but he held back, his greater strength allowing him to control how quickly they went.

More like slowly. He eased into her, stretching her with his girth, filling her with his flesh. She dug her nails into the muscles of his back.

He stopped and trembled.

"Am I hurting you?" she asked in sudden concern, flattening her hands on his back.

"The only way you could hurt me is if you stop."

"Then why are you shaking?"

His gaze, alight with golden fire and desire, caught hers. "I'm shaking because I want you so badly."

A smile tugged at her lips. "Then what are you waiting for?" She locked her legs around his waist and squeezed. Had he truly wanted to, he could have held back, but with a groan of surrender, he let himself be pulled into her welcoming sheath.

He thrust deep, so deep he hit a sweet spot inside, and her channel spasmed around him, squeezing him tight. Sweet heavenly bliss. Hot, passionate explosion.

There were no more words between them as their lips met in a sizzling frenzy that matched the frantic rhythm of their lower bodies.

In and out, he pumped his body, driving his shaft deep and heightening her pleasure. His every thrust drove her closer to the edge, bringing her to the brink of ecstasy, and then he sent her tumbling over.

She screamed his name, "Derrick!" as she came.

And as for Derrick? He came, too, a spurt of wet heat that happened the moment he bit her!

Chapter Nineteen

Nothing ever felt more right than the first time Derrick sank balls deep into Janine. Unless he counted the second time and then the third. Over and over, he claimed her that night, the next day, all that week as she took some time off work for them to explore their new relationship.

And yes, they were in a relationship. *She's my mate now.* And soon, she'd be his wife. He'd already asked for and received permission from Orson and Janine's mother. A conversation that went along the lines of...

"I'm going to marry your daughter."

"I get to plan the wedding."

"I'll have you cremated if you hurt her."

Derrick could already tell they'd fit in well with his family.

Snap.

The clicking fingers brought him back to Janine, who sat on a log and stared at him. Out in the middle of the woods, with a tent set up for the night, they weren't exactly here to camp. Janine was playing doctor again and not the naked kind that involved fixing him with kisses.

"I don't know if I'm ready for this." A lie, since he could feel the pull of the full moon.

"You can't keep hiding from your wolf."

"I'm not hiding," he grumbled. "He is. Ever

since he forced that shift and I was a potato head for a while, he hasn't tried to escape."

Apparently, what happened managed to traumatize his wolf in a way their other experiences hadn't. It also kind of traumatized Derrick. He'd never forget that moment when he thought he'd never move again.

"The fragment is gone now. The doctor said there's no danger if you shift."

"Aren't you worried my wolf might not let me come back? It happens, you know."

"You'll always come back to me." How confidently she said those words now, because they were true.

I'll never leave you, Red.

She trusted him. Time for him now to trust the wolf. After all, that was who he was and always would be.

Come and run, old friend. Let us celebrate being free.

Run they did, on three fleet feet through the woods, chasing scents, across a meadow of long grass following the trails of rabbits. Their speed perhaps was not as nimble on three legs, but the freedom of movement and the thrill of being a predator still felt the same.

When the legs tired, and a rest became needed, they went to find the one with the spring-grass eyes and lay at her feet, waking her from her slumber.

Without fear, she stroked the soft fur between the ears. "You came back to me."

I'll always come back. He was done freakn' out.

Epilogue

An exaggerated groan left Derrick as he heaved Janine out of the car. The sound totally deserved a laser-hot glare. "Are you implying something?" No denying she was a little more rotund these days.

He pulled her close, not caring that her big belly got in the way. A smile tugged his lips as he looked down at her. "I am totally stating that you are beautifully pregnant with *my* child."

"*Our* child."

"It's a girl, which makes her automatically mine. Or haven't you heard the expression?"

Of course she knew it. Daddy's girl. Being one herself, she knew all about that special bond.

"June-bug's here." Orson's happy exclamation had her smiling. He couldn't stem his excitement of the fact that he was going to be a grandpa. A grandpa who would love her children like he loved her and never let them down. *Never leave me.* Much like Derrick would never leave her. He'd vanquished all his demons for a chance to be by her side, and she'd exorcised her demon too.

I'm so lucky. She blinked at the tears brimming and drew Derrick's notice.

Her husband snorted. "Do I need to pull out the handkerchief again already? I don't think it's dry yet from the last waterworks session."

That deserved a slug to the arm. "Don't you

start." Because Derrick did so love to tease her about the tears she couldn't help. Yes, she was a tad more emotional these days, but only because she was so freakn' happy. Sniffle. And it was all his fault. Poke. She jabbed him in the side again, simply because.

"Hey! Isn't that spousal abuse?"

"Talk to my complaint department later." Mood lightened meant, despite her wet lashes, she winked at him before looping her arm in his. He tucked his hand over hers as they turned to walk inside the house, his limp still noticeable months after all the physio, but as he liked to joke, "I totally kick ass in a three-legged race."

Actually, Derrick kicked ass in everything he did. Having survived the war, the nightmares, and rehabilitation, he'd begun volunteering while he worked on becoming a physical therapist. Within the next few years, they planned to open a rehab center of their own, a place where the wounded, mentally and physically, could come to escape the darkness that threatened to swallow them.

The daunting task of starting their own business paled in comparison, though, to the thought of this afternoon.

Hopefully, they would both survive the baby shower waiting for them. By the looks of it, everyone was here, the entire Grayson family and her family and friends. Way too many testosterone-laden shifters in one place, which would probably mean a brawl later on. Good thing they now had a few cops in the family to smooth things over if they got rough.

Family, holy smokes, did she have a ton of

that now, a family that spanned a few generations and meant loud gatherings, lots of talk, food, and love.

Never forget the freakn' love because it made each day worth living.

The End

Here is the complete Freakn' Shifter series:

Delicate Freakn' Flower, Already Freakn' Mated, Human and Freakn', Jungle Freakn' Bride, Freakn' Cougar, Freakn' Out

See EveLanglais.com for more amazing stories.

46796324R00129

Made in the USA
San Bernardino, CA
15 March 2017